Story of the Year

☆

the ten winning stories

THE INDEPENDENT

Story of the Year

☆

the ten winning stories

Susan Akass, Edoardo Albert,
June Burrows, Sarah Harris,
Nicola Jones, Sharon Mead,
Rupert Morgan, Felix Pirani,
Caroline Pitcher, Emily Smith.

SCHOLASTIC

Scholastic Children's Books,
Scholastic Publications Ltd,
7-9 Pratt Street, London NW1 0AE, UK

Scholastic Inc.,
730 Broadway, New York, NY 10003, USA

Scholastic Canada Ltd,
123 Newkirk Road, Richmond Hill,
Ontario L4C 3G5, Canada

Ashton Scholastic Pty Ltd,
PO Box 579, Gosford, New South Wales,
Australia

Ashton Scholastic Ltd,
Private Bag 1, Penrose, Auckland,
New Zealand

First published by Scholastic Publications Ltd, 1993

Text copyright © the authors, 1993

Illustrations copyright © the illustrators, 1993

ISBN 0 590 55510 3

Typeset by A J Latham Ltd, Dunstable, Bedfordshire
Printed in England by Clays Ltd, St Ives plc

10 9 8 7 6 5 4 3 2 1

Contents

Introduction

Writing stories for children is no easy thing, or at least it isn't for most of us! Nevertheless, we received nearly four thousand entries to the *Independent*/Scholastic Story of the Year Competition. That was a marvellous, almost overwhelming response to the most successful competition the *Independent* has ever run (the pile of manuscripts in the Scholastic offices would have made a handsome garden wall!). We would like to thank every single one of the three thousand, seven hundred and twelve writers who entered their stories for helping to make the competition such a resounding success. A team of experienced children's editors had the difficult task of panning through these thousands of stories looking for gold, looking for the best of the bunch. This team managed, after a lot of reading, soul-searching and wrangling, to reduce the four thousand to twenty.

Then it was up to the panel of judges — Michael Rosen, children's writer and presenter of BBC Radio 4's *Treasure Islands*; Julia Eccleshare, children's correspondent of *The Bookseller*; Judge Stephen Tumim, HM Chief Inspector of Prisons; Elizabeth Hammill of Waterstones; Angela Lambert, feature writer and columnist on the *Independent*; and Suggs, lead singer of Madness — to pick the final ten stories and then the winner. Sue Bates, chair of the Federation of Children's Book Groups, represented the views of six to nine-year-olds from schools throughout Britain. They all went at the task with a will, with great deliberation, understanding, enthusiasm and passionate differences of opinion! They were looking for stories with good shape, a beginning, a middle and an end; for well-written stories by writers who have the talent to make words work for them in an exciting way; for stories with a point to them, stories that entertained, were funny, sad, interesting or moving, stories above all that children who have only just learned to read *wanted* to read.

The Story of the Year Competition was started with this simple aim: to draw more attention to the importance of writing stories for early readers – the six to nine-year-olds – and to draw attention in a *positive* way. The so-called 'reading debate' often reaches media as negative. Statistics are produced to say that too many children can't, or don't read. Then some group is blamed, be it writers, parents, teachers, governments, publishers, television programme makers. . . the list is endless.

We believe the news is much better. We are lucky in this country to have so many fine writers for children, and the intention behind the Story of the Year Competition was to celebrate storytellers who produce work for children of this young and vital reading age. That is why the competition was open to all writers, both published and unpublished. And that is why we would like the competition to continue and grow annually. There will be another Story of the Year next year.

Lastly, we wanted to emphasize the importance of stories themselves. Children need stories, people need stories, it's as plain and as mysterious as that. The late William Golding once said that people wanted him to be for them a theologian, psychiatrist, psychologist, priest, historian, archaeologist . . . but that at heart he felt he was simply a storyteller, and what really interested him was the indefinable 'something' that gives a good story its power. In this anthology you will find the ten winning stories in the competition. We would like to congratulate the overall winner, Caroline Pitcher, for the beautiful *Kevin the Blue* and *all* the writers in this book for ten excellent stories, all so well-written and wonderfully varied. We think they all contain that special magic and mystery that makes a good story. What that is exactly, who can say? Maybe *you* know and will enter the Story of the Year 1994. We hope you do. In the meantime, happy reading.

David Fickling
Editorial Director
Scholastic Children's Books

winner

Kevin the Blue

CAROLINE PITCHER

Illustrated by
IAN BECK

This story was written after catching some of Crispin Fisher's enthusiasm.

Harry crept across the kitchen floor. His wellingtons squeaked like a finger rubbing a balloon and she heard him.

"Where do you think you're going, Harry Hodgkin?" she called.

"I'm going to see Kevin," he said and ran out of the back door.

"Who's Kevin?" she cried.

Harry kept on running, across the garden, through the gate, down the hillside speckled with cowslips to the stream.

"She can stay with that baby," he muttered. "I'm going to see Kevin the Blue. He isn't sick on me, he doesn't dribble and he doesn't need nappies. All she ever says is 'Not now, Harry, I'm busy with the baby.' Now I know how my old teddy felt when I sent him to the jumble sale."

On the banks of the stream the willow trees trailed their yellow-green leaves in the water, like girls leaning forward to brush their hair. There were tall plants called policemen's helmets which would have pink flowers, then seed-pods which exploded when you touched them.

Harry settled in his secret den to wait for Kevin.

It didn't look like a den. Three trees grew close together and made a perfect place to hide. Harry kept an old ice-cream box under a root. Inside was half a packet of soggy custard creams and a hat.

It was a fisherman's hat. Harry had found it further along the bank, among the wild forget-me-nots. It was too big so he had to perch it right on the back of his head to see out, but it was a dull green colour and good camouflage.

Harry's other camouflage was silence. There must only be the churning of the stream on the stones.

In the chocolate-brown mud of the bank opposite there was a hole. Harry stared at it for so long that he saw an odd little face grinning back at him, a cross between a goblin and a water-rat. Harry blinked and shook his head.

There was no face after all.

"Come on, Kevin," said Harry. "I'm cold." The willows met over the water as if they were playing 'Here's the church, here's the steeple' and they kept out the warmth of the sun.

Just when Harry thought he couldn't stay still for one more second, a dazzling blue light darted down the flightpath of the stream like a tiny turquoise Concorde, then hovered by the hole in the bank.

Kevin was here!

Of course, it might have been Kathleen, because there were two kingfishers. Harry had watched them flying at the bank, digging out mud with their bills to make a tunnel.

Kevin disappeared inside.

"Perhaps Kathleen's sitting on the eggs and he's brought her a fish supper," whispered Harry.

Seconds later the kingfisher was back. He paused, then whizzed upstream, swift as a stained-glass arrow.

Harry felt a firebomb of joy explode in his chest. It was river magic! He had his very own secret, his king and queen birds. Kingfishers were rare and rich as jewels.

Back home, he sat on the doorstep to pull off his muddy wellies.

"Hello, Harry!" said his mother behind him. "Dad's home. He's looking after the baby so why don't we read a book? Or play a game? We never get a chance to do things together now."

"No thank you," said Harry. She would just have to wait.

He ran upstairs and opened his bird book at the kingfisher page for the umpteenth time. It said that kingfishers laid six or seven white eggs. They hatched after about three weeks. Then the parents fed the fledglings with small fish and water creatures for another three weeks. They would have to rush in and out, stuffing food into gaping bills.

"A bit like Mum and her baby," giggled Harry.

The next day at school, Harry drew kingfishers in his Special Topic book. It was difficult to get the colours right, especially the brilliant blue upper parts with the emerald gloss on the wings and top of the head. Underneath was a chestnut-orange colour like the cinnamon Harry's mum put in apple cake.

Harry wrote about the birds digging out their nest, and then hid his book right at the bottom of his drawer. He didn't want anyone to see it.

Especially David Snaddlethorpe.

Some children were scared of David Snaddlethorpe. He walked with his arms stuck out and he had a big face with little eyes like currants in a Sally Lunn.

David Snaddlethorpe liked birds, but not in the same way as Harry. David Snaddlethorpe collected birds' eggs like other children collect badges or toy cars.

He's like a great greedy cuckoo, thought Harry. If he ever robbed the kingfishers' nest I'd want to kill him.

Just before playtime Mrs Green gathered everyone together for news. John Campbell's stick insect had laid lots of eggs, Judith Pottle had been sick all over the new sheepskin covers in her dad's car, and Michael Stenson's little brother had stuck a coffee bean up his nose.

"How's *your* little brother, Harry?" asked Mrs Green.

Harry said, "I've been down to the stream and found a—"

He stopped. All the children were waiting. He saw David Snaddlethorpe's little eyes fixed on him, hard as burned currants.

"I've found an interesting plant," he mumbled. "It's called policeman's helmet."

David Snaddlethorpe snorted like a pig.

"What a stupid name for a flower," he sneered. "Are the police down there guarding something?"

He looked round to see who thought he was funny. Some children did.

Harry hung his head in shame. He had almost given away his dearest secret, just to show off.

Mrs Green said, "I hope you're careful near the stream, Harry. It's dangerous."

"Mum could hear me scream," he said, thinking, it's the kingfishers who are in danger.

Harry went down to the stream each day on his way home from school. The grass grew long and lush in the spring rain. Harry took an old cycling cape of his dad's to keep in the den. When he put on the cape it was like sitting inside a tepee with your head poking out of the smoke hole.

One afternoon he saw Kevin and Kathleen whizzing in and out with food in their bills and he knew the eggs had hatched. There would be three more weeks before the fledglings were ready to leave.

At school, Harry worked in his kingfisher book but at home those weeks were so boring! Mum and Dad only noticed him when he slammed out of the room or when he was pulling his wide-mouthed frog face. The thing that wound them up most of all was his joke eyeballs on springs. Harry loved to frighten his mum with them, turning round suddenly so that the eyeballs bounced out at her. One night she tore them off and shouted, "These will go in the dustbin if you do that to me again!"

So Harry took them to the den. He made a bird-watcher to keep him company. The silly bird-watcher was made from the cycling cape draped over some branches, with the fisherman's hat perched on top. Harry hooked the eyeballs so that they dangled down beneath the hat. He named the bird-watcher Bobby, so that B.B. could watch K.K. with H.H.

Now it looked as if someone had been

plastering under Kevin's doorway, because the bank was white with droppings. Harry's bird book said that the tunnel would be slippery too, and littered with bones and bits of minnow and stickleback. Every time Kevin and Kathleen emerged they took quick baths in the stream.

That evening Mum said, "Why don't you ask Kevin home to play?"

"He won't be able to come," muttered Harry.

"But you're always on your own," she said.

Rubbish, thought Harry. The kingfishers darted through his mind all the time. He longed for the fledglings to come out into the daylight to learn to fly. That time would be so short. He mustn't miss it. He had a terrible dream. David Snaddlethorpe was waiting for the fledglings too. When they came out he snatched their little blue bodies out of the air and dashed them down into the mud. Harry woke up trembling.

Harry was beginning to like baby-watching as well as bird-watching. The baby noticed him now and Harry was learning how to look after babies. When Mum went to Parents' Evening Harry said to his dad, "You'd better get him clean clothes before she gets back. He's covered in banana and she says it stains."

Dad disappeared for clean clothes. Harry knelt down and brushed bits of banana and soggy biscuit off the baby. He whispered, "I've got a friend called Kevin the Blue. He's a kingfisher and he's got babies. You're the only one who knows, Humphrey."

He sang,

> "Kingfisher blue, dilly dilly,
> Kingfisher green,
> No one but you, little brother,
> Knows who I've seen."

Humphrey gave him a big smile. There was one tooth in his pink mouth, like a sharp, peeled almond.

When Mum came home she looked hard at Harry.

She said, "There isn't anyone in your class called Kevin, is there?"

"No," said Harry.

"In fact there isn't a Kevin in the whole school, is there?"

"Don't think so," he muttered.

She wasn't cross. She said, "Your books are beautiful, Harry. I'm proud of you."

Mum wasn't the only one who had looked at Harry's books. When he arrived at school the next morning he saw that Mrs Green had put his kingfisher book on full display for Parents' Evening. David Snaddlethorpe was peering at it and licking his lips.

"Found a kingfisher's hole have you, Hodgkin?" he smirked. "I knew there was something up. You've been acting sneaky."

"Don't you dare go near it!" cried Harry.

"Will if I like. It's not yours."

"Yes it is! Well, in a way it is. And anyway, they've hatched so you can't steal the eggs."

"I could have the babies though," whispered David Snaddlethorpe. "I've got a stick like a shepherd's crook and it's good for hooking things, specially things out of nests down tunnels. I could keep some chicks in my old budgie cage now the dog's had the budgie. I could get them stuffed and sell them."

"It's against the law to catch kingfishers!" cried Harry.

David Snaddlethorpe just laughed.

Harry could hardly breathe. What could he do? David would go looking for the kingfishers after school. Harry would have to get there first. He must protect them, even if it meant sitting up all night long.

Harry's eyes hardly left the clock all day. To make things worse, a storm was brewing and he began to get a headache.

Just before hometime Mrs Green sent him to the headteacher to ask for more pastels to finish his kingfisher colouring. The headteacher searched for ages and then said, "Sorry, Harry, we must have used them all up."

When Harry ran into the classroom, only Mrs Green was there. Everyone else had gone home.

He fled without even a goodbye, out into the wind and slanting rain, remembering too late that his anorak was still on its peg. The sky was dark and full of storm. On the hillside the long grass soaked his legs. He slipped and fell and rolled to the bottom. He lay there panting for breath. What terrible things had Snaddlethorpe done by now? If he had hooked the babies out of the tunnel they might have fallen in the water and drowned, with poor Kevin and Kathleen fluttering over them, crying in small shrill voices for their children.

"Why didn't I get Mum?" cried Harry.

There was a great splash and an eerie wail.

Harry scrambled to his feet and stared.

David Snaddlethorpe came crashing through the policemen's helmets, setting off a hundred little explosions like bursting pepperpots. He was splattered all over with mud and his eyes stretched wide with terror.

"Bogey man!" he gasped. "Bogey man, lying in wait to get me!"

He staggered past Harry and floundered up the hillside through the long grass. The wind carried his wail, "Bogey man, Bo-gey man . . ."

Harry heard another sound. Flapping.

He hesitated. Then, with his heart beating like a bird trapped against glass, he stalked that sound through the willow trees.

It was coming from his den.

There was a bogey man all right.

It was a bogey bird-watcher called Bobby.

The wind had got inside the cape and blown it out like a balloon and the eyeballs rolled madly.

Harry sank to the ground with relief.

"Thanks for keeping them safe, Bobby," he said.

The storm rolled away and the pale sun swam into the sky.

Harry felt the river magic.

He watched, spellbound.

The little kingfishers came out of the tunnel into the sunlight and clung to the low branches of a willow tree, iridescent as dragonflies.

Then, as if they had been given a secret sign, they burst over the stream in a shower of brilliant blue sparks.

They hovered and returned. Harry tried to count them but they flashed away before he could finish.

Kevin and Kathleen hovered above the water, watching and guiding the flying practice.

"It's like a firework display," whispered Harry. "They're even more beautiful than I dreamed."

He decided there were six fledglings just before they finished their display and vanished into the tunnel.

Harry was exhausted, and happy, and hungry too. He set off up the hill for home.

Someone was coming to look for him. It was his mum, with Humphrey clinging to her side like a baby monkey. Harry grinned.

"Come and meet Kevin, Mum!" he said.

CAROLINE PITCHER

Caroline Pitcher was born and brought up near Hull and now lives in Derbyshire. She studied English and European Literature at Warwick University, and shortly after graduating, moved to London to work for about thirteen years as a primary school teacher. She is now an established full-time writer for children, and has had numerous books published. She has two small children, Lauren (aged seven) and Max (aged four). She has a strong concern for environmental issues, and Kevin the Blue *was inspired by a kingfisher she saw nested on the banks of her tiny local river, the Ecclesbourne. She enjoys reading, writing, cooking and eating vegetarian food, walking and listening to music. She says: "I have always written, as a child, and as a teenager. Now that Max has started school, I have more time. I'm miserable if I can't write. It's the way I understand, find out, celebrate. I want to write all sorts of books for all ages, but feel good children's stories can be enjoyed by anyone, whatever age, at their level. What we read as young children can shine deep inside us for the rest of our lives."*

runner-up

Bogart

RUPERT MORGAN

Illustrated by
PETER BAILEY

To Graham Walker (Wacker) who inspires many little boys.

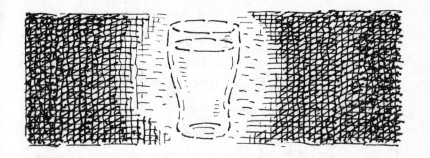

It was late and Bogart was tired. Dog tired and pooped out would be an accurate description. All he wanted was to get some sleep, bag some Zs, forty winks and a little shut-eye — yup, all things considered it was Bo-Peep time for Bogie. Only the kid was keeping him awake again.

He'd figured something like this would happen when he heard him ask for a glass of water before they went to bed. So now he needed to go to the little boy's room. Wouldn't you just know it?

Kids! he thought. *They never learn.*

Of course, if he would just go to the can and do his business they would all be able to go beddy-byes. Crash out and generally hit the sack big time. But the kid couldn't do that —

naturally it couldn't be that simple, could it? He wasn't exactly sure what the problem was here, but he had a pretty darn good hunch.

Something under the bed, I bet . . . he sighed to himself. *Kids*!

Bogart was no stranger to this situation – if he'd had a dollar for every time some kid had kept him awake because of something under the bed . . . well, he reckoned he'd be a pretty rich teddy by now.

Actually, Bogart didn't take too kindly to being called a teddy. He didn't look like a teddy, after all – he wasn't one of those fluffy creampuffs with big button eyes and a dumb grin slapped on their mug the whole day. He was kind of ugly and beaten up – hardly surprising considering the way life had treated him. A guy can't stay fluffy forever, after all. Hang around with kids too long and one day you find you're looking your age, losing your fur . . . next thing you know some lady's sighing over you and saying she'll have to stitch your arm back on. What a life!

Maybe he'd started off as a teddy some time way back when, but to tell the truth he couldn't remember. His memory wasn't too good and it was a fair old stretch since his fluffy creampuff days. Nowadays he was just Bogart — not Bogart the teddy or Bogart the bear, just Bogart the Bogart. He'd seen kids come and go — before this one there'd been his brother, before that the elder sister, then their dad back in the old days . . . and they'd all kept him awake because of something under the darn bed in their time.

He was all tuckered in. Darn it, he wanted to sleep so bad that if only he had a hammer he might just have hit himself over the head with it right there and then, but the kid kept fidgeting and making sort of whiney noises under the covers. Added to that it was cooking up a Sunday roast under there, and the kid was clutching him like they were going to do the tango any minute, so all in all there wasn't any way he was going to get to hit the hay until they'd sorted out this problem.

"*Pssst! Kid!*" he whispered. "*You going to take a leak or not?*"

The kid stopped his whimpering and replied, "I don't need to, Bogart. Not really I don't."

Huh! Bogart had heard that one before. It was the same every time — the first thing a kid always did if he was scared of something under the bed was try to pretend he didn't really need to take a leak. Did they think he was stuffed yesterday?

"*Who are you trying to kid, Kid? Is all this whimpering about an ingrowing toenail or what?*"

He knew he was being kind of grouchy with the little fella, but when a guy needs his winks he can't be expected to behave like a Barbie doll, darn it!

"I suppose I do need to go a little bit, actually . . ." the kid replied eventually.

"*No kidding . . .*" Bogart muttered from somewhere in an armpit.

There was silence following this stunning revelation, which Bogart eventually realised he was going to have to break himself.

"*So what are you going to do about it, Kid? The toilet ain't going to come here, you know.*"

Again there was silence as the kid mulled miserably over this basic shortcoming of toilets, until he announced with little conviction,

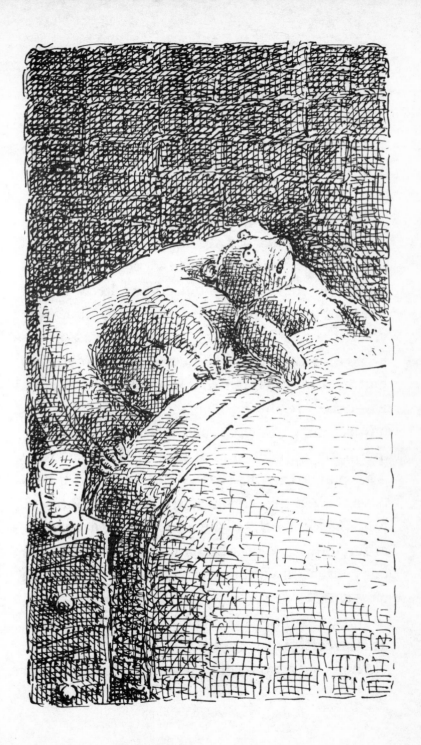

"Maybe I'll be all right. Actually, I don't need to go that bad . . . in fact, I think I'll just go to sleep."

"*Oh no you don't!*" shouted Bogart from the armpit. "*You know what will happen and I ain't standing for it, you hear?*"

"I'll be fine, don't worry, Bogart — I'll go in the morning. Let's go to sleep!"

With this the kid turned decisively around under the covers and buried his head in the pillow. For a while Bogart listened to him as he yawned and tried to pretend that he was on the verge of dropping off to sleep. How many times had he gone through this monkey business? he wondered to himself. If he wasn't so good-natured he'd . . . well, actually there wasn't an awful lot he could do because the kid was quite a bit bigger than he was — but if he could, he'd have shoved that sprog right out of bed and sent him packing off to the toilet without further argument. As it was he had to try and keep his cool — reason with the little guy, talk him round to seeing sense . . .

"*Hhh-hrm! . . . Oh, Kid?*" he asked as calmly and sweetly as he could. "*. . . Kid?*"

There was no reply. Bogart thought about

how to broach the subject tactfully, given that he knew the kid would deny it until he was blue in the face, but he wasn't really much good at being tactful so in the end he just came right out with it and said, "*You're going to pee-pee in the sack, Kid!*"

There was no response except for a slight deepening of his breathing as if he were already asleep and so Bogart carried on, trying as best he could to be reasonable about the whole thing.

"*I mean, I know it's tough and everything, Kid, really I do, but try to see it from my point of view — it ain't you who's going to end up in the washing machine. I hate washing machines, Kid — I get sick! And then I smell like I was going to meet the Queen or something, and you know I ain't that kind of guy. Have a heart, won't you?*"

At first Bogart thought it wasn't going to work because there was still no reply, but in the end the kid, in a very small voice, replied, "I'm scared."

This was not actually news to Bogart, but he held himself back from saying so and suggested,

"There's something under the bed, right?"

The kid nodded miserably under the covers, pulling his feet in a little further at the thought of it. It was a lot more serious than Bogart had thought.

"Anything in the cupboard?" he asked the kid gently.

"Maybe . . ." came the hushed reply.

There was no doubt about it, Bogart realised – the kid had a bad case of the heebie-geebies. One of the most serious spooks he'd come across in a long time. If he didn't find some way of solving the problem he could just about count on getting tumble-dried tomorrow.

Now, although he could be quite short-tempered and although he was something of a realist himself, Bogart knew better than to fob off a kid's fears of something under the bed, especially when there may be something in the cupboard as well. He didn't know the truth about these things himself – maybe there was something there and maybe there wasn't, but the fact of the matter was that a kid who *thinks* there could be something under the bed is not inclined to risk finding out. On the other hand,

he did know that in all his experience of kids —
and he had more experience than most — he had
never, not once in all his time, known one who
had been got by a thing under a bed. He had
come to the conclusion that at the very worst
these things, whatever they were or weren't,
were pretty slow movers.

"I'm scared, Bogart," the kid repeated.

"*I know you are,*" Bogart replied softly. "*I
know you are. But let me tell you a thing, Kid
— I've slept in a lot of beds in my time, known
a lot of kids like you, and they were* all *scared
of something under the bed once in a while, and
you know what happened to them?*"

"No-o . . ." came the hesitant reply.

"*Nothing. Not a darn thing. Take your
brother — he used to think there was something
in the sock drawer as well as the cupboard and
under the bed. Never got him, whatever it was.
And your father — heck, I remember when he
used to wave me outside the covers as bait just
to see if the coast was clear, and I'm still here,
ain't I?*"

"Dad used to do that?" the kid asked
in amazement.

"Don't tell him I told you, but he sure did — and I used to have one heck of a time getting to sleep afterwards, let me tell you. Thing like that makes a guy pretty jumpy, know what I mean?"

There was an impressed silence. Bogart hoped that he had convinced the kid it was safe for him to go, but he wasn't sure — kids always had a nagging fear that there might be a special thing under the bed that only wanted *them* and no one else. Darn, it was hard getting to sleep some nights!

Eventually there was a very, very quiet whisper in his ear. Quiet so as not to alert the things under the bed to what was going to happen.

"Will you come with me, Bogart?" he asked.

Bogart thought about this for a second. Now, the fact of the matter was he was bow-wow tired and tempted to go through the whole shenanigan of getting out of the warmth, hanging around in the toilet while the kid did his business and getting settled all over again just so long as he could be sure of getting his sleep. But on the other hand . . .

"No, Kid — you've got to go on your own.

If there's anything under there you've got to show it that you're not scared, and that way it'll never get you. Heck, why do you think these things never hang out under grown-ups' beds? Because grown-ups aren't afraid of them, that's why! I tell you, you show them one time that you ain't scared and they'll never bother coming back — presuming they're there in the first place, which ain't ever been scientifically established."

"Do you really think so?" the boy asked tremulously.

"I know so, Kid. I been through this before, you know."

There was a short pause, and then Bogart felt a hand sliding across the sheets to pull back the covers.

"Don't jump, now," he warned. *"You put your feet right there on the ground just to show them you ain't scared . . ."*

Again the kid paused, as if this was really too much to ask, but eventually he slipped his legs slowly over the bed and placed them on the floor. He stood up, and then walked slowly out of the room.

Bogart was proud of him. That was a pretty brave kid when you got right down to it.

When the boy came back he got calmly into bed again, feeling as if he had just beaten off every bad thing in the world. He put Bogart carefully on to the pillow beside him and rolled over to go to sleep.

"*We going to get some winks now, Kid?*" he asked.

"Yeah . . . thanks, Bogart," the boy replied, sleepily.

"*Don't mention it — just doing my job. Sleep well, now.*"

The boy drifted off and Bogart was left alone, wide awake all of a sudden. He was feeling a little sad. Although everything he'd said had been the truth, there was something he hadn't told the boy: when kids stopped being afraid of things under the bed they fairly soon stopped needing him in bed with them. He knew it would only be a matter of time — a few months, a year or two — before he found himself being left on the floor by mistake all night long, and one day he would end up back in the cupboard. It was always the same.

Kids! he sighed to himself.

Just as well there was the little sister in the cot next door.

STORY OF THE YEAR

Rupert Morgan

Rupert Morgan was born in London, and now lives on a Dutch barge — the Albatros — *which at present is at no fixed mooring, somewhere in Europe! After graduating from Manchester University, he worked for two years as an Account Manager with an advertising agency in London. He was one of* The Spectator *Young Writers of the Year finalists in 1988, and the winner of the* Elle *Short Story Talent Contest, 1989. He has subsequently had articles published in* Elle, The Spectator *and the* Guardian. *His first full-length novel is sitting in a publisher's office, waiting to be read!* Bogart *is his first published work of children's fiction. He enjoys travelling on his barge and has a large collection of comics. He says: "When I was a child I had an invisible friend called Mr Bonjy. I imagined him to be somewhat fat with a big, rather clumsy body — I think it was because he was embarrassed about it that he stayed invisible. He was a very kind-hearted and long-suffering chap who never got angry with me, but he always wanted a quiet life and found the company of children quite exhausting. I don't know where he came from or where he is now, but this story's character, Bogart, is to a great extent that invisible friend of my childhood."*

runner-up

The Jack Fruit Tree

NICOLA JONES

Illustrated by
NICK SHARRATT

To Lenny, Anna and Simeon.

Anna was looking out of the window, waiting for her grandpa to arrive. He had been on holiday for a long time and she was looking forward to seeing him again. She was just getting rather tired of waiting and had started breathing on the window and writing her name, when she saw him coming down the road. He had his Sunday hat on and something round and green, about as big as a pumpkin, under his arm. Anna ran to the door and opened it.

"Grandpa, you're back!" she said, giving him a big hug.

"Yes, my dear," Grandpa said, his eyes twinkling, "and look what I've brought you all the way from Jamaica."

"What is it?" asked Anna. She poked a

finger at the big green object. It felt quite hard and rough.

"That's a jack fruit," said Anna's grandpa, "the queen of all Jamaican fruits. I picked it just for you yesterday morning, before I got on the plane."

A jack fruit is a magic fruit. It tastes a bit like peaches and a bit like melons. It's sweet like honey and smooth like cream. It's a little bit crunchy and it's a little bit soft. Some people say it tastes like every fruit you've ever had, all rolled into one. One of the most surprising things about a jack fruit is its seeds. They're quite big and shiny brown and fit snugly into your hand, like a flat pebble you might find on the beach.

Anna and her grandpa went into the kitchen. Grandpa put the jack fruit on the table.

"What does it taste like?" Anna asked.

"Would you like me to cut you a piece?"

"Oh, yes please," said Anna.

Grandpa took a knife and cut into the jack fruit. He carved a big slice for Anna and took out the seeds. The fruit was pale yellow, the colour of bananas. Anna opened her mouth wide and took a big bite. It was delicious and she was quiet for a while as she ate up every bit. When she finished she looked at the jack fruit. She had eaten a large piece and she felt full, but there was still a lot left.

"There's enough jack fruit here for everyone in my class to have a piece," she said to her grandpa. "It must have come from a very big tree."

"Yes, Anna," he said. "It's tall like a giant and it's fat like an elephant."

"Is it taller than our house?" Anna asked.

"Taller than a church," said Anna's grandpa.

Anna tried to imagine a tree that big. The tallest trees she had ever seen were in her cousin's garden in Wales, but they were poplar trees and didn't have any fruit.

"Grandpa," Anna said, "what does a jack fruit tree look like?"

Grandpa looked at her over the top of his glasses, his brown eyes thoughtful. He took out his pen and drew a picture of the tree on the edge of his newspaper. It had big leaves sticking out of the top, and a wide trunk. It looked a bit like a fat palm tree.

"It's something like this," he said, "but I can't draw it well. When I was a boy we had a tree like this in our backyard. When a jack fruit fell down we used to fill up our bellies with the fruit."

"Didn't your mum mind?" asked Anna.

"Only if we didn't eat the food she cooked for us," chuckled Grandpa.

Anna tried to imagine Grandpa's backyard in Jamaica. In her garden there weren't any fruit trees, only roses and a few plants that she wasn't supposed to touch. Grandpa's backyard had mangoes and bananas and star apples and custard apples, and when you put a stick in the ground, it grew into a tree.

The piece of jack fruit that Anna's grandpa brought her from Jamaica had five seeds. She put them on the table and looked at them. She remembered the bean seeds her class had planted at school that had grown into bean stalks, with big hairy leaves and lots of white roots.

Anna picked up one of the seeds and looked at it closely. At one end she could see it was splitting a bit, showing the bright green flesh inside. A little pointed bit was beginning to poke out of the split. It was starting to sprout.

"Look, Grandpa, it's starting to grow," Anna said.

"So it is, Anna," chuckled Grandpa. "Perhaps you'd better plant it and then you will be able to see what a jack fruit tree looks like."

Grandpa got up from the table and put on his hat. "It's time for me to go home and unpack," he said. "Ask your dad to help you plant that seed."

"Goodbye Grandpa," Anna said. "And thank you for bringing me the jack fruit."

When Dad came home from work that night, Anna showed him the seeds.

"Yes, Anna," he said. "I remember them when I was small. We used to take the seeds and roast them and eat them. They taste like nuts."

"I don't want to roast mine though, Dad, I want to plant them and grow a jack fruit tree as tall as a giant and as fat as an elephant," Anna said.

Dad laughed and went to the garden shed. He brought back a flowerpot and some of the special soil he used for growing seeds, and helped Anna to plant the seed that was sprouting. Then he popped the pot inside a plastic bag and put it on the central heating boiler.

"In Jamaica it's very warm," he said. "That's what jack fruit seeds need to make them grow."

Every day Anna came back from school and looked into the pot, but nothing seemed to be happening. She watered the seed and waited. One morning she woke up to the sound of her dad's voice saying, "Quick, Anna, get up! Come and see your jack fruit tree! It's grown in the night!"

Anna ran downstairs. An amazing sight greeted her. In the flower pot was a huge green sprout, nearly as long as her arm. The little polythene bag was sitting on the top, looking like a flag on the top of a flag pole. Dad scratched his head. "I don't believe it!" he said. "Last night when I went to bed there was nothing, but now look at it! You must have green fingers, Anna."

Anna looked at her fingers, with a worried expression. To her relief, they were the same colour they'd always been. Her mum was in the kitchen making her packed lunch for school. When she saw Anna looking at her fingers she laughed. "Don't worry, Anna," she said. "It's just an expression which means you're good at growing things."

The little pot wasn't big enough for the plant any more. The roots were sticking out of the holes in the bottom. Anna's dad brought in a large bucket of soil from the garden. Anna helped him take the small jack fruit tree out of the little pot very carefully. It had lots of knobbly roots. Anna didn't like them much. They looked like long white worms. They put the tree in the bathroom, where it was warm and light.

That night Anna was very excited. She wondered how big her jack fruit tree would grow by the morning. She couldn't wait to see what Grandpa would say.

In the morning Anna got up and went to the bathroom to clean her teeth. She was sleepy and had forgotten about her jack fruit tree. She had some trouble opening the bathroom door. It seemed to be stuck. She pushed it open as far as she could and squeezed in. Then she saw what was blocking the door. Her jack fruit tree had certainly grown in the night! The trunk was so big it took up nearly the whole bathroom. She couldn't even get past it to the basin. She looked

up. There was a big hole in the roof where the jack fruit tree had grown right through it. Above her Anna could see some large leaves waving gently in the breeze, and beyond that she could see the blue sky. A pigeon was perched on one of the branches, preening itself in the sunshine.

"Mum! Dad!" she shouted. "Come quickly! Look what's happened."

Her dad poked his head round the door. He looked up at the tree. "Goodness me, Anna! What have you done? Just look at the roof! How are we going to stop the pigeons coming in?"

Her mum squeezed in through the door.

"Never mind the pigeons, how are we going to clean our teeth?" said Anna's mum. "I can't even get to my toothbrush."

"It's not my fault," said Anna. "Don't blame me. I only watered it every day, like you told me."

"The tree is too big for us to carry outside now," said Dad, looking up at the leaves high above their heads. "We'll have to think about what to do."

"You aren't going to cut it down, are you?" asked Anna anxiously.

"Of course not," Dad replied. "There's

always a solution to every problem. Let's go downstairs and have a think about it over breakfast."

Whilst they were eating their toast and puzzling about what to do, Grandpa knocked on the door. Anna ran to let him in.

"Grandpa, Grandpa! Come and see what we've got in our bathroom," Anna said as soon as she saw him.

"Well, well," he said, when Anna showed him the tree, "I never thought I'd see one of these growing in England. It must be a magic jack fruit tree! We'll have to move it somehow. It's a tropical tree and it doesn't like the cold. It won't last too long out there. It's really messed up the roof, hasn't it? That hole will have to be fixed before it rains."

Anna didn't want her tree to die. She didn't want it to be chopped down either, but she knew that you couldn't really live with a tree growing through the middle of your house.

That night Anna lay in bed thinking about the jack fruit tree. As she was going off to sleep she suddenly remembered something. Her jack fruit tree wouldn't have to die after all! She knew just the place where it could grow tall as a giant and wide as an elephant and still keep warm.

In the morning she told her mum and dad about her idea.

"Do you remember when we went to that park with that huge greenhouse in it?" she asked. Mum and Dad looked a bit puzzled.

"You know, the place where all the banana and mango trees were growing, just like in Jamaica," she explained.

"Oh yes," said Dad, "now I know where you mean. What a good idea, Anna. The tree would be quite at home there. Just let me make a phone call."

Dad was on the phone for quite a long time and came back smiling.

"It's all fixed," he said. "Someone is coming to pick the tree up tomorrow."

The next day a man arrived in a big lorry with a crane on the back. His name was Mr Francis. He was small and round and looked quite important. Mum explained that he was a tree expert who knew all about trees, especially those which grew in Jamaica.

By this time the tree really was as tall as a giant and as wide as an elephant and all the neighbours had come to see it sticking out of the roof. Someone was even taking photographs for the local newspaper. Mr Francis walked about the front garden looking up at the tree and writing things in his notebook. Sean O'Sullivan from next door leaned over the fence and said to the man, "What are you going to do with that tree, mister?"

"We're going to put it in a special greenhouse in a place called Kew Gardens. It's a fine specimen and the only one of its kind in the country. You'll be able to come and see it there," Mr Francis replied.

Mr Francis went into the house and squeezed into the bathroom. He tied ropes around the jack fruit tree to fix it to the crane. Then he went down to his lorry and pulled the levers in the cab of the lorry and the jack fruit tree was lifted up through the roof and lowered gently on to the trailer, without damaging a single leaf. Everyone who was watching cheered as the tree reached the trailer safely, and Mr Francis gave a little bow.

Anna felt a bit sad as she waved her tree goodbye, but she knew it was going to a place where it could grow very big. The glass house at Kew Gardens was as tall as a church.

A week later Anna and her mum, dad and grandpa went to visit the tree at Kew Gardens. It had grown even taller and looked spendid with its large green leaves. It had been planted between two banana trees. Beneath it was a special plaque that said, "This tree was grown and donated by Miss Anna Philbert." Anna felt very important and proud when she read it.

"It looks just like my backyard in here," said Grandpa. "I feel like I'm back home in Jamaica."

"Now I know what your backyard looks like," Anna said.

"Yes," said Grandpa, smiling, "but next time I go to Jamaica I think I'll bring you a pomegranate. Pomegranate trees are much smaller and won't make a hole in the roof."

STORY OF THE YEAR

NICOLA JONES

Nicola Jones is married and lives in Camberwell, South London. She has two small children: Simeon, who is five, and Anna, who is seven. She studied African History and Social Anthropology at the University of London, and then took a PGCE and taught in secondary schools for twelve years, as an English teacher, and as a Special Educational Needs teacher with bilingual pupils. She is now a part-time lecturer at a London college, on their English PGCE course. She is actively involved on the management committee of a project called the Hummingbird, which organises crèches, after-school care and holiday schemes for children in North Peckham, and she regularly writes articles for the Independent. *She says: "The Jack Fruit Tree is about my daughter Anna, who is seven. It is the first story I have ever written and she helped me to write it. She read it and told me which bits were funny and which bits were boring and what I should do to make it better. The story I wrote is based on real life. Anna did plant a jack fruit tree and although it didn't really grow through the roof it is sitting on our window-sill at home."*

Princess Chocky

SARAH HARRIS

Illustrated by
SUE HEAP

With love to Mum and Dad.

Princess Chocky was one of a kind. She wasn't an ordinary princess like Cinderella. She didn't want to hang around waiting for a handsome prince to turn up, she just wanted a big piece of chocolate fudge cake.

Her sister, Princess Beauty, was a pretty average princess. She sat around all day wearing a white frilly dress, combing her long blonde hair and filing her nails. Princess Beauty ate salad for breakfast, salad for lunch and salad for tea. To Princess Chocky's horror she wouldn't touch chocolate. Princess Beauty wanted to fit into her mum's wedding dress, so she had to stay slim.

Princess Chocky was an unconventional princess. She would never be caught dead wearing a frilly dress. Dungarees were much more practical for chasing goblins and ghouls.

Chocky had bashed hundreds of bad fairies. She had sometimes been a little too enthusiastic and bashed a couple of good ones as well.

Bashing fairies was hungry work, so Chocky would munch her way through a couple of chocolate fudge cakes every day. She didn't care if they made her fat. They were just so yummy.

Poor Chocky was a disappointment to her mum and dad. King Blighty and Queeny had rather hoped for a boy, so he could go off on a quest and rescue a rich princess. They didn't mind if she was an ugly princess, she just had to be stinking rich.

King Blighty and Queeny were a very poor king and queen. They had to pay a huge rent on their castle to Rumpelstiltskin.

By day, Queeny sat around doing nothing and smiling graciously. By night, she ironed hundreds of shirts to earn some extra money. Despite her efforts, Rumpelstiltskin had threatened to throw them out of Fairytale Land unless they paid him a whopping big pot of gold.

While Chocky was climbing a tree somewhere in a very un-princess-like fashion, her mum and dad were having a serious conversation.

"We have to earn some money and pretty darn quick," said King Blighty, frowning. "It's time our daughters got hitched, tied the knot and all that romantic business. They have to marry rich princes and get oodles of money. Then you'll never have to iron another shirt again, Wifey."

Queeny thought this was a brilliant idea and thumped King Blighty on the back. She detested ironing. She also disliked washing Chocky's dirty clothes every night, as she was always falling into some river and getting muddy.

"I'll hire a fairy godmother to find a bewitched frog," said Queeny. "Our girls can kiss the frog and it'll turn into a very rich prince."

"Fiddlesticks!" snapped King Blighty. "I'll put an advertisement in the lonely hearts column of the *Fairytale* newspaper."

King Blighty and Queeny received hundreds of replies from all sorts of princes for Princess Beauty. They had to turn some very handsome ones away because they just weren't rich enough.

Princess Beauty wasn't too bothered who she

married. After all, one rich prince is very much the same as the next.

She eventually picked Prince Haughty. He was very wealthy and liked eating salad, so they ate radishes together happily every after.

King Blighty was pleased he had got rid of one daughter and earned a big pot of gold. He now wanted to see Chocky happily or unhappily married so he could go on a safari to Kenya with Queeny.

"But nobody'll want to marry our Chocky," wailed Queeny. "She eats too much chocolate fudge cake. We'll never find a prince to marry a fat princess unless we pay him, and we can't afford to do that."

"Don't fret, love," said King Blighty. "Chocky will just have to go on a diet. I'll forbid her to eat a piece of cake ever again."

"No way, Dad!" shouted Chocky, who was swinging upside-down from a tree. "I'm not going on a diet for a stupid prince. If I'm not allowed to eat chocolate fudge cake here then I'm off."

"You'll do no such thing!" shouted King Blighty. "You're so selfish. Think of your poor mother. Do you think she likes washing and ironing hundreds of shirts? Anyway, I've solved the problem and found a prince who's not too fussy.

"His name's Prince Lentil and he's a health-food fanatic. He's going to swim 100 lengths of his swimming pool, jog 200 kilometres and then cycle over 500 kilometres to see you. He should be here by lunch-time tomorrow."

"I'm not marrying a fitness fanatic!" cried a horrified Chocky. "There's no way on earth I could live happily ever after with a wimp who doesn't eat chocolate fudge cake."

"You'll grow to love him," said Queeny a little uncertainly. "Look at me and your father. I detested him to begin with. When I kissed the frog and it turned into your father I cried with disappointment, but look at us now."

"What do you mean?" said King Blighty crossly. "I was very good looking."

"You can say what you want but I'm not going to marry him," said Chocky firmly. "If you want me to go on a diet just to marry a weed who eats carrots all day, I'm going."

"Fine!" shouted King Blighty. "I wash my hands of you if you won't do as I say. Go and find your own fortune and don't come asking me for pocket money."

"Goody gumdrops!" laughed Chocky. "I can't wait. I'm going to have hundreds of adventures and chocolate fudge cakes."

Chocky had a quick game of football with the servants and then packed her rucksack full of chocolate fudge cake. She climbed on her bicycle, waved goodbye to her mum and dad and then pedalled off as fast as she could before they changed their minds.

She had a brilliant plan. She wouldn't wait for a stupid prince to turn up when he felt like it. She would go and capture one for herself.

Chocky had read in the Lost and Found column of *Dragon News* that there was a reward of £500 for the return of Prince Lost, a rich prince who had vanished. I'll find him, no problem, thought Chocky. Then I'll start my own chocolate fudge cake factory.

Prince Lost was an unusual prince. He found it rather a bore having to go off and rescue damsels in distress. They were always so stupid and weepy. What's more, he always got lost trying to find one.

He wasn't too popular with princesses anyway. Not many princesses like having to wait three days to be rescued.

Prince Lost made mistakes, but this one was an absolutely whopping big one. He had been sent off on another mission to kill a dragon and rescue a beautiful princess in a nearby country.

Five days later, Prince Lost began to suspect he had taken a wrong turning four and a half days back. He had well and truly lived up to his name. He was absolutely, undoubtedly and spectacularly lost.

He had ridden for so long he had in fact travelled out of Fairytale Land and was now very near Brighton pier.

Another thing about Prince Lost was that he was incredibly gullible. He saw a sign in the window of a Bed and Breakfast which read: "Kidnapped princess inside needs rescuing. Apply within."

Unfortunately for him, he believed it.

"Great snowballs!" thought Prince Lost. "This is easy. I'm actually in the right place for once. That's nice of them to put a note in the window to help me."

He knocked loudly, feeling very pleased with himself. The old wooden door creaked open.

"What do you want?" a voice croaked.

"I'm a handsome prince," lied Prince Lost, "and I've come to rescue the princess from the dragon or witch or ogre or whatever it is."

Suddenly an old, gnarled hand reached round the door, hooked the prince by his collar and dragged him inside. The door banged shut.

This was the last time Prince Lost was seen. His poor horse, Buggins, stood waiting for him for a day and was eventually horse-napped and made to give children rides on Brighton beach.

Prince Lost had been kidnapped by Dire the Desperate witch. She had been trying to find another husband for years. Not many men came near her, and if they did they met an awful fate. The ugly witch liked to eat her husbands at the wedding feast.

Dire the Desperate witch had been thrown out of Fairytale Land and ended up in Brighton, where a large number of equally unpleasant man-eaters lived.

There aren't many men left in Brighton. The sea air makes men taste a lot nicer so they are quickly snapped up by greedy retired witches for a succulent supper.

Poor Prince Lost was soon to be coated in pastry and popped into a hot oven to be served with newly boiled potatoes and carrots. Chocky was his only hope.

There can't be many princes or princesses braver than our little heroine. She wrestled dragons, slew sea monsters and chopped giant worms in half in her quest to find Prince Lost.

After four weeks on the road, fighting ghouls and everything else that crossed her path, Chocky was tired and fed up. Her bicycle had got a puncture and she had eaten the last of her chocolate fudge cake supplies.

She just wanted to find the blasted prince so she could go home and set up her own business.

Luckily for her she met the big bad wolf on the border of Fairytale Land. He was feeling very sorry for himself since nobody liked him after the way he had treated the three little pigs.

"Everybody hates me," he barked. "I can't live here any more. I'm going to leave Fairytale Land. I'll follow Prince Lost. He was heading for Brighton. Maybe they treat wolves better there."

"Brighton!" exclaimed Chocky. "Holy chocolate fudge cake! He definitely needs rescuing."

Chocky pushed her bike past the miserable wolf and headed for Brighton. She soon found people wearing silly 'Kiss Me Quick' hats on Brighton pier.

A gleaming white horse on the beach caught her eye. He looked like a fairytale horse. Buggins the horse was not very happy at all.

"Wait until I see that stupid prince! I'll kick him up the backside," neighed Buggins. "I hate these horrible children. If I have to give any more revolting little sprogs a ride I'll buck them off."

"Don't worry," whispered Chocky. "Tell me where he is and I'll rescue him and come back for you."

"It's about time," whinnied Buggins moodily. He tossed his mane in the direction of the Black Magic Bed and Breakfast funeral parlour.

Chocky braced herself for the danger ahead and charged. She stopped in her tracks as she came to the front door. There was a rather delicious smell of food wafting out of one of the upstairs windows.

"Mmm," thought Chocky. "I've got time for a quick snack before I rescue that stupid prince."

She swung herself into the tree, climbed on to the window ledge and dropped into the empty room. The kitchen was a bit of a mess. There was flour and bits of pastry everywhere.

"Yum, yum! There might be a jam tart around somewhere," thought Chocky. "*And* there's not a soul in sight to stop me eating it!"

Unfortunately there weren't going to be any jam tarts. The pastry was to make a Prince Lost pasty.

Poor Prince Lost had been fattened up for the last month by Dire the Desperate witch. She liked her men nice and meaty. Poor Prince Lost wasn't very meaty. It didn't matter how much he ate, he never got any fatter.

Dire had got fed up waiting for him to become nice and plump. She wouldn't be able to make a nice family-sized meat pie out of him so she decided to settle for a small pasty with gravy for her lunch. She'd even baked a nice syrup steamed pudding for dessert.

Chocky's carefully trained eye scoured the empty room and spotted the huge steamed pudding bubbling in a pan on the stove. In a flash she moved in for the kill.

After five helpings she began to feel a lot better. It wasn't really worth leaving a scrap so Chocky polished off the last of the pudding and custard.

Just as she was wiping the last drop of custard from her chin, Dire the Desperate witch burst through the door, dragging Prince Lost by the collar.

Her large bristled chin dropped when she saw Chocky. Her yellow teeth snarled.

"You've eaten my pudding, you little wretch! I'd been looking forward to that after my pasty. I'll eat you for that. You're nice and fat. I'll make a big meat pie out of you and freeze the leftovers."

"Not on your nelly!" shouted our plucky little heroine. "You're history, you ugly old hag!"

Seizing a nearby rolling pin, she biffed the witch on the head.

"Take that!" shouted Chocky gleefully. "And that!"

Chocky danced around the witch, scooped up a handful of flour and chucked it in her face.

"You'll regret calling me fat!" she shouted. With an almighty shove she pushed the witch into the big pudding bowl and threw the rest of the flour over her. That put paid to Dire the Desperate witch!

"You saved my life!" gasped Prince Lost, planting a massive, sloppy kiss on her cheek.

"Yeuch!" Chocky shouted and biffed him over the head with her rolling pin.

"Ouch!" shouted Prince Lost. "There's no need for violence like that. You need to be taught a lesson."

"I'll do what I want!" shouted Chocky, picking up a handful of flour and throwing it over him.

"Oh, no you won't!" laughed Prince Lost, picking up a spoonful of syrup and pouring it over her head.

The biggest food fight in the history of Fairytale Land began in earnest. Chocky and Prince Lost were soon covered from head to toe in jam, cream, mustard and pickle. They had great fun.

"You look ridiculous!" roared Chocky.

"Not as funny as you!" shrieked Prince Lost.

Even though Princess Chocky was an unconventional princess, she did have a happy ending. She and Prince Lost became great friends and biffed each other happily ever after.

They built a chocolate fudge cake factory which went bankrupt after a couple of years. They never actually sold any cake but ate it all themselves.

Then they retired to a little cottage by the sea, where they could have as many food fights as they liked without the neighbours complaining.

Now you have to admit, Princess Chocky had a much more exciting life than Cinderella and the Sleeping Beauty put together!

SARAH HARRIS

Sarah Harris is twenty-two and graduated from Nottingham University with a degree in English Literature. She recently took a diploma in Journalism at Cardiff Journalism School, and was a student adviser for Cosmopolitan magazine as well as contributing to the Rough Guide to Berlin 1993. She is now working at the Western Daily Press in Bristol as a trainee reporter and is pursuing a career in journalism. An avid cinema and theatre-goer, she also enjoys travelling abroad – this year she will be travelling to Germany as a guest of the German Embassy after winning a writing competition. Princess Chocky is her first published story for children. She says: "I love writing, especially for children, and find that my most active critics are the next door neighbours' children!"

The Voyage of Out-Doing

SUSAN AKASS

Illustrated by

PADDY MOUNTER

For George, Ben and Frances.

Carl and Christopher lived next door to each other. They were friends of a kind. They couldn't do without each other, but they couldn't do much with each other either. They always had to out-do one another.

When Carl rode his bike, Christopher had to ride his faster. When Christopher shot an arrow, Carl had to shoot one more accurately. When Carl made a den, Christopher had to build a bigger one, and when Christopher collected stamps, Carl had to find ones which were more rare and exciting than Christopher's.

Their houses were near a park. It wasn't much of a park, just a square of tired grass, but it ran down the side of Devil's Hill which was the steepest hill in town. This hill was the scene of some of Carl and Christopher's fiercest contests.

When they were small, the boys had run races down the hill. They had run until their legs were a blur, and sometimes they had tripped and rolled over and over to the bottom. When they were older, they had ridden their bikes hell-for-leather down the hill and had burnt out their brakes trying to stop. In later years they had roller-skated, sledged, scooted and skate-boarded down the hill, and they had scars on their knees, bottoms, elbows and foreheads to prove how seriously they took these races.

Now Carl had a new idea. One day, Christopher heard banging coming from Carl's garden, so he looked over the fence. Carl had tools and timber scattered all over his lawn.

"What are you building?" asked Christopher, after watching silently for a few minutes.

"None of your business," replied Carl.

"Are those pram wheels going on it?"

"What if they are?"

"I've got it! It's a go-cart!"

"It might be."

"And so might the thing *I've* been planning for the last few days, except that mine is a four-wheel drive, turbo-charged, injection-fuelled, off-road vehicle, not just a go-cart."

"I don't care what you call it. It won't beat mine!"

"Want a bet?"

"You're on! At the hill, this time next week?"

"Done! This time next week!"

For a week both gardens echoed with the sounds of sawing and hammering, muttering and cursing. The two boys worked in almost total secrecy with only the occasional peep over the fence. They raided their sheds, their lofts and their cellars for wood and wheels, for chains and ropes, for nails and pulleys, for pipes and wires, for nuts and screws and oil and glues. They puzzled and planned and tested and tried, until exactly one week later they whistled their secret whistle across the fence. They were ready for the race.

Carl and Christopher pulled their perfectly designed go-carts to the top of the hill, sat down side by side and wedged their heels firmly into the grass.

"Are we ready? . . . Go!" they shouted.

With a kick and whoop they were off,

bumping and clattering down the hill, faster and faster, tearing the turf, scattering dogs, sending seagulls screaming into the sky. There was a dip and a mound halfway down the hill, cause of many a spectacular accident in former races. They hit it at nearly thirty miles an hour and for three seconds both were airborne, before landing again with a bone-rattling crash. Unscathed they raced on, neck and neck, lying low and streamlined with never a thought about how they would stop.

Each hit the fence at the bottom of the park at exactly the same moment, and at exactly the same moment they were both catapulted from their go-carts and flew over the fence to land, simultaneously, in the brambles on the other side.

They did not even argue about it. They knew, as they picked the prickles out of one another's bottoms, that it was a perfect dead heat. Thoughtfully, they pulled home the crumpled and splintered wrecks that had once been their go-carts.

"Same time next week?" said Carl.

"Same time next week," agreed Christopher.

The boys were back to their drawing boards, this time in total secrecy. Each had to make an improvement to the design of his go-cart that the other could not guess at, for neither could rest easy until he had beaten the other. And so there was a period of silence in the gardens as each thought and thought about winning modifications. Then the banging began again, along with some curious roarings and splutterings and the odd minor explosion.

Race day arrived and the two go-carts were pulled from the secrecy of the two garden sheds where they had been kept under lock and key and twenty-four hour surveillance. They were now somewhat larger and heavier. They had unrecognisable bits sticking out, some hinged, some on springs, some double-reinforced and some packed under covers. The boys peered curiously at each others' vehicles but made no comments as they heaved them to the top of Devil's Hill.

Preparations for the race took longer this time. Back to back, maintaining their secrecy, the boys fiddled with screwdrivers and tinkered with spanners. Then they checked gauges and meters that had been attached to rather similar new control panels on both go-carts. And this time both boys had helmets to put on and seat belts to fasten.

"I'm ready," said Christopher at last. "Prepare yourself for a shock. You're not going to believe this when you see it."

Carl tightened the chin strap on his bicycle helmet.

"Nothing you've made can out-do what I've engineered," he laughed, sounding supremely confident.

"Right! Are we ready? Let's GO!"

With a kick they were off, bumping, rattling and gaining speed, and again they were neck and neck, burning the grass beneath their wheels. The mound was approaching. Each boy gritted his teeth and, as each hit, there was a roar from his machine, jet engines fired and the go-carts rocketed into the air. In an instant wings sprang out from the bodies of the vehicles, no longer go-carts but jet scooters flashing above the house tops.

Carl and Christopher looked at one another in amazement.

"You spied on me!" screamed Carl. "It was my idea!"

"Never!" bellowed Christopher, "I would never stoop so low. I worked it all out from first principles."

"But the wings! They're almost the same!"

"Inspired by the laws of aerodynamics . . ." shouted Christopher.

"And made from packing cases and sofa springs," replied Carl. "But the jets! What are yours powered by?"

"Solar power, of course. What about yours?"

"Methane gas collected from fermented guinea-pig droppings."

"So yours will run out of fuel! I'll win! Mine will travel on for ever!" shouted Christopher triumphantly.

"Only until the sun goes in!" retorted Carl.

"There's not a cloud in the sky!" laughed Christopher as he increased the thrust of his engine with a touch of a button.

"You can't get away from me!" shouted Carl and he opened the throttle so that his jets screamed with power.

They sped on in close formation, shouting

above the roar of the jets as they tried to out-do each other over the brilliance of their machines.

"Mine has sprung wheels for landing," Carl boasted.

"Well, mine has a parachute for a slow descent."

"I've got bags of emergency provisions."

"And I've got a compass for navigation."

They didn't notice anything about their flight. They didn't see the patchwork fields far below them, dotted with tiny sheep and cows, or feel the rush of the wind through their hair. They didn't see the excited groups of people pointing upwards, convinced they were aliens in UFOs. They noticed nothing until the throaty roar of Carl's engine faltered and spluttered. At the same moment, a big black cloud blew across the sun and the pleasant purring of Christopher's engine wound down into silence.

They looked down and then they looked back at one another with horror. They were miles from home. They were flying high over the sea!

"We're going down!" screamed Carl. "We'll plummet like stones into the ocean. It's the end of us!"

"No it's not! Release your parachute," shouted Christopher, pulling his ripcord.

"I haven't got one," wailed Carl. "I'm done for!"

"No! Grab on to my wheel," yelled Christopher. There was no time for Carl to unstrap himself from his seat. He just stretched out and grabbed on. A huge yellow parachute filled with air and slowed the plunging descent of the two go-carts. But they were still going pretty fast. They didn't have time to argue about anything before the ocean was racing up to meet them.

"Brace yourself for impact!" screamed Christopher. Carl let go his grip on Christopher's go-cart, they curled in their seats, hands around their heads and hit the water, splat!

"Now we're going to sink!" wailed Christopher. "Release your seat-belt and swim for your life!"

"Sink? Never!" shouted Carl joyfully. And with a whoosh, four huge air bags inflated around his go-cart. "Climb aboard!" he called to Christopher.

Spluttering and gasping, Christopher swam

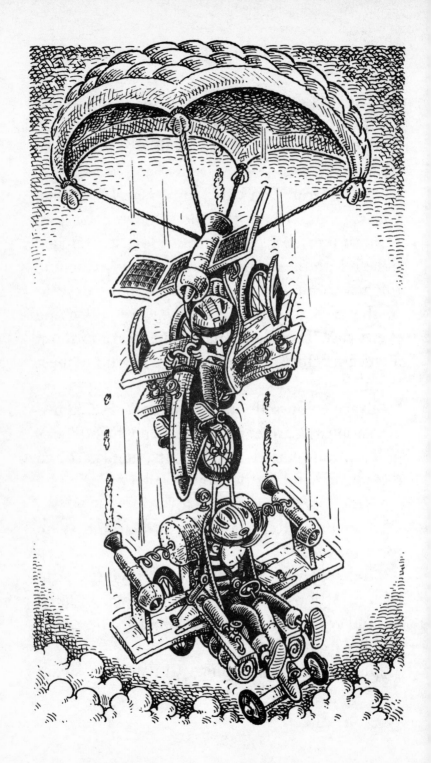

over and heaved himself out of the water. He flopped into the seat with Carl and watched as his beautiful go-cart slipped slowly beneath the waves, pulling the great yellow bedspread parachute down after it.

"Pity . . . that was a good machine," conceded Carl, "I liked the parachute. Putting that in was good thinking."

"Your air bags are pretty good too. Did your mum know you'd used your camping air-beds?"

"Not exactly. But she said we weren't going camping this year so she won't discover till next year. Did your mum know about the bedspreads?"

"Well, she had said she wanted some new ones."

The boys sat quietly for a while, munching chocolate biscuits from Carl's emergency rations. The little craft bobbed on the waves and the breeze blew them slowly towards land. Then Christopher said, "Who won the race?"

"Why, I did of course! I've still got my go-cart and you haven't!" said Carl with surprise.

"But if it hadn't been for my parachute, you'd have been smashed to smithereens and scattered across the ocean," snapped Christopher.

"True," said Carl, "but you'd be shark food if it hadn't been for my air bags."

"But you'd have been smashed to smithereens *before* I was shark food," argued Christopher.

"Something might have happened to stop me going down."

"Like what?"

"Like a whale might have caught me on the jet from its blow-hole."

"Fat chance! Where's the whale?"

"Then a whirlwind might have sucked me into the clouds."

"And I might have been carried safely home on a dolphin's back, without your silly air bags!"

The argument continued, becoming more and more ferocious, and neither boy noticed that they were being driven towards a wild coastline of cliffs and jagged rocks. But as he paused for thought, Christopher suddenly saw what was happening.

"Carl, stop talking and look!"

Carl looked hastily around. The cliffs were looming large and the roar of the waves filled their ears. There was nowhere to land.

"There's no hope this time," said Christopher.

"Yes, there is! My rescue flare!"

"Where?"

Quickly Carl pulled a plastic bag from under the seat. In it was a box of matches and a rocket (lost mysteriously the previous bonfire night). He leant forward and inserted the rocket into a launch tube on the front of the go-cart, then lit the touch paper. There was a fizz and a hiss and the rocket shot up and exploded in a star-burst of colour against the darkening sky.

Would anyone see it? It was their only hope. Furiously, the boys used their hands to paddle away from the rocks, but their efforts were futile against the strength of wind and tide. They were only metres away from the rocks when they spotted the helicopter circling out from the cliffs. As they waved and screamed, it paused, hovering above their heads, and a coastguard was lowered on a rope. He seized them, each under a brawny arm, and they were hoisted skywards. But as they rose into the air Carl began to struggle in the coastguard's grip. "My go-cart!" he yelled in dismay. "Don't leave my go-cart!"

The coastguard couldn't hear much above the

racket of the rotor blades, but he was surprised that Carl wasn't more grateful to be snatched from certain death. He put the boy's reaction down to shock and, in a way, he was right. For Carl *was* shocked, but only about losing his go-cart. Once the boys were safely inside the helicopter he muttered to Christopher, "If I'd got it home I'd have been the real winner, whatever you say."

"But you didn't, did you?" retorted Christopher, as he sipped tea provided by the disgruntled coastguard. "So it's another dead heat."

"I suppose so," sighed Carl.

"Same time next week, then?" said Christopher, eagerly.

"Same time next week!" agreed Carl, brightening up.

The helicopter swooped back over the cliffs and landed at a remote coastguard station. There, the two boys were hustled into a police car which rushed them home, sirens blaring.

And did Carl and Christopher enjoy all this fuss and excitement? Did they describe the thrills and spills of their epic voyage to the policewoman who accompanied them? No! All through the journey home they sat in silence, eyes screwed up with concentration, planning how to out-do each other in their Mark Three go-carts.

STORY OF THE YEAR

SUSAN AKASS

Susan Akass lives in Bath and has two children, Frances, aged four and Ben, six. She read English at Oxford University, and then taught primary school children for eight years, which includes three years in Australia. She has had several stories published in Playdays *magazine, and has written for BBC Children's TV. Her first children's picture book was published this year, and has been sold to six countries. She says: "I took up writing a couple of years ago during a career break from teaching. Reading with children in schools and studying children's literature for an M.Ed first gave me an interest in children's books, but having my own children gave me the time and inspiration to start writing. Now my children give me ideas, act as guinea-pigs for my stories and help keep me in touch with children's books of all kinds."*

Mayor Bumble's Proclamation

SHARON MEAD

Illustrated by
MARTIN BROWN

To Dan and Tommy and Mary.

Mayor Bumble was a busy man with many plans. In Greenfort he was a hero, having raised the little town from poverty to prosperity. What had once been dusty tracks were now tidy streets, and once poor peasants were now wealthy farmers. But Mayor Bumble was not yet done.

"It is not enough," he announced to his council one day.

"Whatever do you mean, Mayor Bumble?" asked the council.

"We have peace," said Mrs White.

"And prosperity," said Mr Park.

"Yes, yes," Bumble replied dismissively. "We have peace and prosperity. But," he added, with a gleam in his eye, "we have no rest and repose."

"But, sir," said Mrs White, "I am sure I rest daily."

"And I," said Mr Park, "I am certain I repose nightly." He demonstrated his luxurious manner of repose.

"Of course you do," said the mayor. "When you can."

Mayor Bumble swept to his feet and punctuated each point with a gesture.

"Have you never been bitten by a mosquito at night?" he demanded. "Have you never thrashed in vain as it whines about your ear?" He slapped and thrashed for their edification.

The councillors nodded. Of course they had.

"Have you never been stung by a bee, bitten by a spider, or bled by a leech so that the throbbing of your wound keeps you awake at night?

"And," he continued, "if a citizen's dog has fleas, how can that citizen rest at ease?"

The councillors were properly impressed.

With that, Mayor Bumble handed down a proclamation, as follows:

Proclamation the First

Inasmuch as creatures having more legs
than four or fewer legs than two are sometimes injurious, often pestiferous, and always
disgusting, for the rest and repose of the good people
of Greenfort, all aforementioned creatures are
hereby prohibited

Well, it is a measure of the esteem in which he
was held that Mayor Bumble was immediately
obeyed. The bees buzzed angrily away, the
earthworms and snakes wriggled off to greener
pastures, and the spiders unslung their webs.
Before long, not a gnat was to be glimpsed or a
fly to be found anywhere in Greenfort.

It was glorious. Mayor Bumble was twice the
hero he had ever been, and if rest and repose
had not been so much in the air, the celebrations
would certainly have continued all night.

When the new day dawned, the prosperous
farmers of Greenfort worked their fields
contentedly, free from worry about cornborers
and grasshoppers. From now on they would
have perfect, bountiful, luxuriant crops.

The householders of Greenfort found no

potato beetles munching in their gardens, no mealworms eating their flour, no cockroaches infesting their kitchens.

The children of Greenfort romped giddily after school in fields free of wasps, ticks, and snakes.

Even the pets and livestock were happier, now that they were free of fleas and tapeworms.

But late in the afternoon a humble fisherman appeared and asked to speak with the mayor.

"Please, Mr Mayor," he began, "I hesitate to disturb your rest and repose . . ."

"Have no fear, sir. What troubles you?" said the mayor. In the light of his recent triumph, he was prepared to be especially gracious.

"Well, sir," the fisherman continued, "it's just that there are no fish in the river."

"What?" said the mayor. "Wherever can they have gone?"

The fisherman shuffled nervously as Mrs White whispered in Bumble's ear.

"Oh, yes, of course," said the mayor reassuringly. "Have no fear, it will be attended to."

And immediately the mayor issued an order for his proclamation to be amended:

Proclamation the First
(Amended)
Inasmuch as creatures having more legs
than four or fewer legs than two are sometimes injurious, often pestiferous, and always
disgusting, for the rest and repose of the good people
of Greenfort, all aforementioned creatures are
hereby prohibited. Except fish.

The problem having been settled, the mayor sent
for his afternoon tea. In due course, Mr Park
arrived with a pot of tea and some lovely scones
and crumpets. The mayor buttered a scone and
reached for the honey pot, only to find that
there was none.

"Park, you've forgotten the honey!" he said.

"No, sir," came the reply. "There are no bees,
so there is no honey. Fancy some jam?"

Well, Bumble most certainly did *not* fancy
some jam, but he made do with good grace. Then
he immediately issued another amendment:

Proclamation the First
(Amended) (Again)
Inasmuch as creatures having more legs
than four or fewer legs than two are sometimes injurious, often pestiferous, and always
disgusting, for the rest and repose of the good people
of Greenfort, all aforementioned creatures are
hereby prohibited. Except fish. And honeybees.

"We shall have to hope that they behave themselves and refrain from stinging people," he mused, as he made his way into his garden for a little rest and repose.

There, he found his wife hoeing vegetables.

"Well, my dear," he said, settling himself on a bench, "I trust you have rested and reposed comfortably today?"

"Yes, Bumble dear," his wife replied. "The garden is ever so much less work now."

Bumble smiled contentedly.

"But you know, my pet," continued Mrs Bumble, "I rather miss the butterflies. And I think many of the birds have nothing to eat now. Perhaps they will leave as well?"

"Well, I am sure, my love," the mayor replied stiffly, "we shall have to do without them."

"Of course, dear."

Just then a small Bumble dropped out of the apple tree at his father's feet. "Papa," he said, "why are there no ladybird beetles to play with? Surely you cannot have sent *them* away as well?"

"Well, I suppose I have," his father said. "But that is a small price to pay, don't you think?"

"Yes, Papa."

Then another Bumble called out from a group of children digging in the meadow. "Papa," she cried. "There are no worms to dig for fishing!"

"Blasted fish again!" Mayor Bumble harrumphed. "They are a troublesome lot!"

And the next morning the following notice appeared in the town square:

Proclamation the First
(Amended) (Yet Again)
Inasmuch as creatures having more legs than four or fewer legs than two are sometimes injurious, often pestiferous, and always disgusting, for the rest and repose of the good people of Greenfort, all aforementioned creatures are hereby prohibited. Except fish. And honeybees. And worms and ladybird beetles. And butterflies.

In the days that followed, the fishing was good and the butterflies returned, greatly to the benefit of rest and repose in the Bumble household. But the ladybird beetles, requiring aphids to eat, chose to stay away despite Mayor Bumble's invitation for their return.

And then another curious thing happened.

"Mayor Bumble, Mayor Bumble!" An old

woman hailed him from the street.

"What is it now?" Bumble muttered as he made his way to the gate. But aloud he said, "Can I help you, Mrs Potter?"

"Mayor," she said, "excusing my assault on your rest and repose, sir, but the caterpillars are crunching my cucumbers. There's no stopping them. They breakfast on broccoli and lunch on the lettuces. Soon I shall have no garden left!"

It was true. Where there are butterflies, there will be caterpillars, and where there are no spiders, beetles, or mantises, there will be *many* caterpillars indeed.

Encouraged by Mrs Potter, a small crowd began to gather around the mayor.

"What are you going to do, Mr Bumble?" cried one. "I've lost all my petunias and begonias."

"And my cabbages have not a leaf left!" added another.

Alarmed by the angry tone of the crowd, Mayor Bumble retired to the safety of the town hall to consider the question.

"What shall we do, councillors?" he said. "I expect we shall have to get rid of the butterflies again. I should not have given in to my wife's

soft heart."

"But sir," said Mrs White, "butterflies help the bees to pollinate our orchards and gardens. Perhaps we are better off with them than without them."

"Not if they eat everything in sight," said Mr Park. "I begin to fear they will eat the dog!"

"Oh, dear!" said the mayor.

"But that is not all, Mr Bumble," said Mrs White. "We have trouble in the grain fields and granaries. Mice and rats by the millions are devouring every seed they can discover."

"Bah!" said Bumble. "We shall buy cats and set traps."

"But the farmers have done so, sir," said Mr Park. "It has helped only a little. They now demand a goodly supply of snakes."

There was no help for it — Mayor Bumble would have to add a new list of 'excepts' to his glorious proclamation. But as he began to consider it, the list grew ominously long.

"Let's see," he thought. "If we take away the butterflies, the fruit won't get pollinated and the birds will go away. Or if we except the spiders, mantises, and beetles, will the caterpillars be enough to feed them? And . . . good heavens, I forgot about the snakes!"

Before long, the 'what ifs', 'howevers', and 'what abouts' jumbled together in his mind until his rest and repose were sorely tried.

"Enough!" he said at last. "Mr Park, take down a new proclamation."

The next day, the troubled townspeople gathered in the square to read the following notice:

Proclamation the Second

Inasmuch as creatures having more legs than four or fewer legs than two are sometimes injurious, and often pestiferous, but nevertheless necessary to the rest and repose of the good people of Greenfort, they are hereby declared a protected public treasure. Moreover, they shall not be considered disgusting.

STORY OF THE YEAR

SHARON MEAD

Sharon Mead is living temporarily in Norwich with her husband, Dan, and two children. Their permanent home is in Carlisle, Pennsylvania. She was born in Wyoming, USA and studied anthropology at Columbia University in New York, specialising in Chinese culture. At the moment she is working in England as a freelance Chinese translator, and a writer — she has had non-fiction general interest articles published in American regional magazines, but this is her first published children's story. She enjoys reading, gardening and softball, and has recently taken up karate. She says: "My nine-year-old son Tommy and seven-year-old daughter Mary are a good critical audience for my stories. I admire many children's writers, but the greatest influence on Mayor Bumble's Proclamation *was Charles Dickens. Having just read* Our Mutual Friend, *my mind was full of Dickens' musical phrasing, and this story flowed out in just under five hours. I particularly admire stories that, through their humour and style, entertain children and adults alike. That is the kind of story I try to write."*

Abigail on the Tow-Path

Felix Pirani

Illustrated by
Debi Gliori

For Abigail and her brothers.

Abigail decided to walk to the end of the world.

"It's quite a long way," said her father. "I'd better pack you some sandwiches." And he did: two cottage cheese and one strawberry jam. He also put in two chocolate bars, just in case.

Abigail put the package in her knapsack, with her map of the world, and set off along the tow-path beside the canal.

Soon she came upon an old woman sitting on a bench. A big black dog was lying on the grass next to the bench. The old woman had only one leg and the dog had only three. Abigail walked a little nearer to the edge of the canal.

"Don't worry," said the old woman, "he doesn't bite."

Abigail stopped. "I shan't worry — I've been

going to self-defence classes," she said. "What happened to your dog's other leg?"

"We both had beautiful stainless steel legs once," said the old woman. "But we lost them overboard in a storm at the end of the world, with all our belongings."

"I'm on the way to the end of the world myself," said Abigail.

"Watch out for unicorns along this tow-path," said the old woman. "They can be fierce. And be very careful if you meet the sandwich-board man. You'll need more than self-defence if you run into him. He's round the bend. He can't tell a mile from a minute. You never know where you are with him. You'll need a map."

"I have one," said Abigail. "And I've never seen a unicorn, but I know what they look like. There's a picture of one in our book of fabulous beasts. My father bought it when he started breeding phoenixes."

"Fiery birds, they are," said the old woman. "The sandwich-board man has one too. It burns up and comes alive again every seven years."

"It can't be much of a phoenix, then," said Abigail. "The best breeds take five hundred years.

My father keeps his in a special fireproof phoenix-coop." She walked off along the tow-path.

Further along the canal, Abigail came to an old barge moored to the bank. A tall bald man was sitting in the stern of the barge, playing a trumpet. There was a white animal standing very still behind him, which might have been a horse, except that it had a silver horn coming out of the middle of its forehead. It was more likely to be a unicorn.

"Hello," said the tall bald man. "What's your name?"

"Abigail," said Abigail. "What's yours?"

"Big Max," said the tall bald man.

"Isn't that a unicorn?" asked Abigail. "I was told to watch out for them."

"Yes it is," said Big Max. "She used to tow barges to the end of the world. But all the barges have engines now, so who needs a unicorn? They're very expensive to feed."

"I thought unicorns lived on air and sunlight," said Abigail. "That's what it says in our book of fabulous beasts."

"There hasn't been enough sunlight here for

years," said Big Max, "so they started bringing it in boxes from California. It got more and more expensive. Have you ever tried to buy a box of sunlight? You can't get one now for love or money.

"This unicorn doesn't need any," he went on. "She's asleep, spellbound by a handsome prince. She's supposed to sleep for another sixty-nine years. But sometimes she wakes up for an hour or two, when I play the trumpet, and then she can be a bit fierce."

I suppose unicorns sleep standing up, like horses, thought Abigail.

"If she came too alive I could hypnotise her," she said. "We learnt hypnotism at Drama Class."

"Who told you to look out for unicorns?" asked Big Max. "I suppose it was the old woman with the dog. I expect she told you that they'd lost their legs overboard in a storm, too."

"Hadn't they?" asked Abigail.

"Of course not," said Big Max. "They lost them in the floating dice game at the end of the world."

"I'm on the way to the end of the world myself," said Abigail. "And I don't want to lose

anything. I'd better eat my sandwiches now."
She sat down on the end of the barge and took
them out of her knapsack.

"Speaking of sandwiches," said Big Max,
"Watch out for the sandwich-board man. He
mixes up space and time. Ask him where, and
he'll tell you when, ask him when and he'll tell
you where. If you listen to him you may lose
your way, and end up two thousand light-years
from home."

"I have a map," said Abigail, "and a watch."
When she had finished the last sandwich, she
stood up and said, "I'd better be getting on." The
sound of the trumpet followed her along the canal.

Round another bend Abigail found the sandwich-
board man. He had a board in front and two
behind, held up by a complicated system of
straps, and he looked very like a sandwich himself,
squashed between his boards. A bedraggled green
bird with a long tail was perched on his shoulder.
All the boards were covered with lettering.

SINNERS REPENT
THE END OF THE
WORLD IS NIGH

"Now I'm getting somewhere," she muttered to herself. "If it's nigh it can't be far."

"What's that?" said the sandwich-board man, turning to look at her.

"How far is it to the end of the world?" asked Abigail.

"Next Tuesday, it'll be, at eleven in the morning," announced the sandwich-board man. "When the trumpet sounds."

"You're mixing up where and when," said Abigail. "Just what I was told to expect."

"I'm not mixing up anything," said the sandwich-board man. "I can tell a mile from a minute. I suppose you've been talking to the old woman with the dog. Or Big Max. He'll play that trumpet once too often, he will. He probably told you that his unicorn used to tow barges. It never did. He won it in the floating dice game at the end of the world. Loaded dice, I expect. That unicorn is stuffed. Not like my phoenix. This is a real one." And he pointed up at it.

"I don't know what that is," said Abigail, "but it's not a phoenix. My father breeds them, so I ought to know what they look like."

"It annoys him when people say he's not a

phoenix," said the sandwich-board man, "so you'd better be careful."

"I was the under-nines trap-shooting champion last year," said Abigail, "so *he'd* better be careful too." She walked round the sandwich-board man, and on down the tow-path.

Soon Abigail came to the canal basin full of barges and boats. On one side was a house, and in front of it a tall post with a signboard fixed to it. On the signboard was a picture of a globe. Underneath the globe it said WORLD'S END.

The globe looked very much like the one on her map. "Here I am at last!" she said to herself.

There was a barge moored opposite World's End. Five people with green eyeshades were kneeling on the deck at one end, playing with some dice. At the other end there was an enormous pile of odds and ends. To one side of the pile there was a kitchen sink, and what might easily be a stainless-steel leg sticking out about halfway up.

That must be the floating dice game, thought Abigail. She walked on to World's End. The front door was closed. Pinned to the door there was a cardboard sign which said "Closed for redecoration. Reopening next Tuesday."

"Oh, bother!" said Abigail to herself. "Here but not here. Or anyway, not now."

She must have said it aloud, because one of the dice-players looked up and said, "Here but not here. That's a good turn of phrase. One good turn deserves another," he went on. "Would you like a roll of the dice?"

Abigail walked over to the barge. "My father told me not to gamble until I was earning my own living," she said.

"It's different here at the end of the world," said one of the other players. "You can't lose, You can only win. That's not gambling."

"What do I have to do?" asked Abigail.

"Just roll the two dice," said the first player. "If the spots add up to seven or eleven, then you win everything in that pile of odds and ends. If they don't, then you have to roll again. And then it all depends."

Abigail picked up the dice and rolled them on to the deck. One came up three, the other four.

"A natural!" said one of the other players. "It's all yours, whenever you want it." And he waved at the pile of odds and ends.

"Thank you," said Abigail. "Isn't that a stainless-steel leg?" She pointed up at it.

"Yes," said the first dice-player. "There's a person's one, and a dog's one, too. They're yours now, along with all the other stuff. Everything but the kitchen sink."

Abigail thought, I'll be able to give the old woman and the dog their legs back. "That's great!" she said. "But why not the kitchen sink?"

"It has to be put back in the kitchen, of course," said the first dice-player. And he waved his hand at World's End.

Abigail looked at her watch. "I'll come back for the legs and some of the other things next Tuesday," she said. "I have to go home now."

She walked around World's End. On the other side there was a road, and not far along the road there was a bus stop. When a bus came along, she climbed to the top deck. She sat at the front, looking out of the window and eating her two chocolate bars.

"Did you get there?" asked her father, when Abigail arrived home.

"Yes, I did," she said. "It was quite far, just as you told me, and there were a lot of people along the way. But when I got there it was closed for redecoration. It opens again next Tuesday. And I won a barge-load of odds and ends in a floating dice game."

"Good," said her father. "On Tuesday I'll come with you, and we'll sort out the bits you want."

STORY OF THE YEAR

Felix Pirani

Felix Pirani was born in London, and has lived there most of his life. He has four children, one of whom is called Abigail, and some grandchildren. He studied at Cambridge and the Carnegie Institute of Technology, Pittsburgh, and is Emeritus Professor of Rational Mechanics at the University of London. He has published many scientific papers and popular articles about Einstein's theory of relativity and others about nuclear strategy and about the environment. Since he retired in 1983, he has written several children's books, two of which feature the character Abigail. He tries out his stories on his grandchildren. Despite this precaution, one story was condemned by a Parliamentary motion for inciting children to alcoholism and violence!

The Reluctant Eagle

EDOARDO ALBERT

Illustrated by
KAY WIDDOWSON

To my parents.

One day the Reluctant Eagle decided he would like to see outside the nest, which was perched on top of a high cliff.

Mr and Mrs Eagle had warned him to be good, and the Reluctant Eagle had promised on the Egg and the Wind. At the time he had meant it, but sitting in the eyrie looking up at the clouds rushing by, he began to wonder what was Out There.

For a moment he remembered his promise, but then he thought to himself that it would be all right just to look. After all, he knew his feathers were not quite ready for flying. If the truth be told, maybe the fact he was doing something he was not supposed to made it more exciting.

Foot by foot he struggled out of the eyrie. By

the time he got to the edge his legs were aching.

Then he had his first look Out There.

It was just as well the eyrie was old and well built so it could take the impact of an almost fully grown eagle falling into it flat on his back.

The sky and cliff had still not stopped spinning around when Mrs Eagle returned to the nest.

"Are you all right, dear?" she asked.

The Reluctant Eagle struggled upright and tried to bury himself under his mother. But he was far too big for that any more and all he succeeded in doing was nearly pushing her out of the nest.

"Calm down, dear. Now, what's the matter?"

"I . . . I looked Out There," the Reluctant Eagle said. "I'm really sorry, I know I promised to be good, but I just wanted to look."

"At least you were sensible enough not to try to fly before you're ready."

"It's so far down, so far down," he said.

"What's so far down?" Mrs Eagle was beginning to realise what her son was talking about.

"Everything. Out There. It's all down."

"But you will soon be able to fly, dear. Up and down, and round and round."

The round and round bit was a mistake. The Reluctant Eagle groaned and hid his head beneath his wing.

Mrs Eagle's suspicions were now confirmed. Hard though it was to believe, her son was scared of heights. For the first time in a long while Mrs Eagle was flummoxed.

Mr Eagle arrived at that moment. When Mrs Eagle had explained what was wrong he prodded his son with his beak and said, "Pull yourself together, boy. This is no way for an eagle to act."

"I wish I'd never hatched." The voice was still muffled as the Reluctant Eagle had discovered that if he kept his head under his wing and his eyes tight shut then everything stopped spinning. "I liked the egg. I never asked to be an eagle. Why couldn't I have been a . . . a rabbit or a deer or something?"

Mr Eagle was too shocked to answer. How could an eagle want to be a rabbit?

Mrs Eagle spread her wings, indicating that her husband was to follow.

"We'll be back soon, dear," she said. "Don't forget to eat your dinner."

The wind caught her wings and in one soaring,

swooping arc she was carried over the cliff to a high crag. Mr Eagle followed.

"How are we going to teach our son to fly if he's afraid of heights?" asked Mrs Eagle.

Mr Eagle was taken by surprise at this request to start thinking so soon after landing. "Er, I think we have to do something," he said.

"So do I," said Mrs Eagle.

"You do? Oh, of course you do. Yes, we have to do something."

"Quite," said Mrs Eagle.

"Right. I know, I'll tell him to start acting like a proper eagle."

"But you already have," Mrs Eagle pointed out.

"Oh."

"Who do we know who's afraid of heights?"

"No one on my side of the family," said Mr Eagle.

"I didn't mean eagles."

"Who else is there?"

"Well, you know."

"I do? Oh, yes, of course I do." Mr Eagle stared off into the distance, hoping for inspiration. He noticed a pairs of ears twitching against the skyline. "Rabbits?" he said.

"Well, not just rabbits," said Mrs Eagle. "Any of the four-feet. They can't fly so I suppose they must be scared of heights."

"Right. Quite. Scared of heights. Hmph!"

"So we could ask them."

"Yes." The word was out of his beak before he could stop it. "Ask the four-feet?"

"Who else would know?"

"Er, yes." Mr Eagle was trying to work out how he had agreed to this.

"So," Mrs Eagle turned to look at him, "what are you waiting for? A watched egg never hatches, you know." As she spoke her wings opened to their full span and before Mr Eagle could say anything she was airborne. He watched her disappear over the edge of the cliff.

"Ah, well," said Mr Eagle and went off in search of four-feet.

Mr and Mrs Rabbit were having a relaxing afternoon nibbling the summer grass when they spotted the shadow.

Hearts pumping, they peered out of their burrow.

"What's he doing here?" whispered Mr Rabbit.

"Ahem!" said Mr Eagle from the entrance to the warren.

The rabbits shuffled backwards.

"I apologise for dropping in unexpectedly like this," said Mr Eagle. "Very bad manners, I know."

"Oh, that's quite all right," said Mr Rabbit, trying to get a bit further back.

"Could you come into the light where I can see you?"

"Er, we're fine here, thank you. Sir."

"Right," said Mr Eagle. "This is just a social call, Mr and Mrs Rabbit. You know, doing the rounds, that sort of thing."

Mrs Rabbit, always a believer in the social niceties, shoved her husband forward. "Ask him if he wants to come in," she whispered.

"Come in?" squeaked Mr Rabbit in horror.

"Thank you for the invitation," said Mr Eagle, "but I really don't think I could fit."

"No, no, he couldn't fit, couldn't get in," babbled Mr Rabbit. He was finding this all a bit too much.

Mrs Rabbit pushed her husband out of the way and came to the edge of the burrow. Brave rabbit that she was, even she could not bring herself to venture out into the open.

"We're very pleased to see you, sir," she said. "And how is the young eagle?"

"Ah," said Mr Eagle and leaned closer to the burrow. "Well, actually, that was the reason I came to see you." Mr Eagle took a deep breath. "I hope what I am going to ask you will be kept in the strictest confidence?"

"Of course," said Mrs Rabbit.

"I knew I could trust you. That's what I say to Mrs Eagle: you can always trust a rabbit. Now, perhaps you can give me some advice. You four-legs, you can't fly, not like we can. So we thought, that's Mrs Eagle and I, we thought that maybe you might be just a touch worried by high places. Am I right?"

Mrs Rabbit nodded.

"That's what I thought. So, we were wondering . . . You see, there's this young eagle we know, a distant relative, cousin twice removed on Mrs Eagle's side of the family, actually. Well, word has reached us that he's well, scared of heights. Won't leave the nest, that sort of thing. And I was wondering what you did with rabbits who are scared of heights?"

"Your . . . cousin has vertigo?"

Mr Eagle nodded.

"Your cousin twice removed?"

"That's right."

From behind her Mrs Rabbit could hear strangled noises as Mr Rabbit pushed his front paws into his mouth to keep from laughing. She could feel her own whiskers beginning to twitch.

"Can't help you there, sir," she managed to say.

"Oh. You're sure?"

Mrs Rabbit nodded. Behind her Mr Rabbit was in danger of exploding.

"Oh, well, thank you very much. And please don't mention this to anybody."

Mrs Rabbit shook her head.

"Goodbye, then," said Mr Eagle.

She waved.

Mr Eagle spread his wings and flapped vigorously a couple of times. When almost out of sight he glanced back and saw the two rabbits lying on their backs by the entrance to their burrow apparently having some sort of seizure.

"Myxomatosis," he said and shook his head sadly.

Through the rest of the day Mr Eagle tried speaking to the other four-legs but the response was the same with them all. No one could help his cousin twice removed. And the curious thing was they all seemed to be suffering from some sort of breathing difficulty. Very strange.

Discouraged, Mr Eagle landed on a tree. It was raining. Water slowly collected at the point of his beak and fell off. Maybe he should try asking the deer? No, not the deer. He would never be able to live it down. They put on enough airs already.

"Fine evening, don't you think?" said a voice.

"Oh, yes, yes," Mr Eagle grumbled.

Mr Fox, for it was he, sat on his haunches and looked up at the eagle. He was grinning.

"And how are you doing?" Mr Fox asked.

"Oh, well, thank you." If there was one animal who made Mr Eagle feel, well, a little uncomfortable, it was Mr Fox. The rest of the four-legs and the wings knew their places. But Mr Fox just grinned his red, red grin.

"Must be a good view from up there?"

"Oh, well. So, so."

"Ah, you're most fortunate. What I would not

give to see the sights you see! But," Mr Fox's voice dropped to a whisper, "should I reach such a height as you're sitting on right now, by my whiskers, I would fall right off."

"You're scared of heights?"

Mr Fox grinned his red, red grin. "Terrified, Mr Eagle. Terrified. But don't you be telling anyone."

"No, no, of course not. In fact, there's a small matter you might be able to help me with."

"Would that be your cousin, sir? Twice removed? On your good lady wife's side, I believe?"

Mr Eagle sat up straight and stiff on the branch. "Who told you? I demand you tell me."

"Demand, do you?" Mr Fox's tail twitched over the ground. "Well, I guess I shall be moving right along then." He turned, and without seeming to move at all was suddenly standing on top of a rock twenty metres away.

"No, wait! Wait." Mr Eagle glided after him, landing just short of the rock. He stood on the sodden turf, rain trickling from his feathers and his beak. "Can you help?" he asked.

Mr Fox grinned. "It will be getting dark soon

enough. That's no time for an eagle to fly. But tomorrow — ah, tomorrow!" Mr Fox sniffed the wind. "Tomorrow will be a fine day for flying. Goodbyeeeee!" His farewell trailed into the distance for Mr Fox was gone.

Mr Eagle's head emerged from beneath his wing into a bright and clear morning.

Then he saw them lined up at the bottom of the cliff. Four-legs and wings all looking up at the eyrie. Even the red deer had come.

Mr Eagle pushed a talon into Mrs Eagle's back.

"Mother!" he hissed. "Mother, wake up!"

"What's the matter . . .? Oh." She stared down at the crowd.

"What's happening, Mother? What's happening?" The Reluctant Eagle pushed his way out from beneath her — really he was far too big to be brooded but he had been so miserable yesterday that she had let him come under her wing for the night.

"Fine morning, is it not?" said a voice.

Three eagles turned to look.

There, standing on the edge of the eyrie, on

top of a sheer cliff where no four-legs had any right to be, was Mr Fox.

"How . . . How?" Mr Eagle stuttered.

"And how are you today, sir? This must be your son. A fine figure of a lad." Mr Fox curled his thick bushy tail around himself and sat down.

The young eagle, remembering his manners, said, "How do you do, sir?"

"And well spoken too. Why, he is a credit to the both of you." Mr Fox leaned closer and whispered. "Well, young fellow, it seems you have an audience. How many eagles can say that the first time they fly? All those four-legs and all those wings — why, they all wish they were you."

"Do *you* wish you were me?" asked the Reluctant Eagle.

"Ah, clever as well as handsome!" Mr Fox winked a big, slow wink. "Shall we show them all just how clever?"

The Reluctant Eagle said nothing.

"You see, over there, in the sky," Mr Fox pointed with his nose and the eagle stared where only eagles can stare, into the heart of the sun.

"See him smiling at you?"

The Reluctant Eagle saw the bright, bright face hidden in the sun.

"Don't you want to go and say hello?"

The Reluctant Eagle nodded.

"Well, you can, you know."

The Reluctant Eagle stood up on the edge of the eyrie. And then he made a big mistake. He looked down again.

"Oh, no!" he said and closed his eyes tight shut.

So he did not see Mr Fox uncurl his long red tail and stand up. He did not see Mr Fox walk around the edge of the eyrie with nothing between him and all the animals on the ground, hundreds of metres below. He did not see Mr Fox put his long red snout right against his ear.

"Boo!"

The Reluctant Eagle jumped.

He fell.

"Open your eyes!" Mr Fox shouted after him. "Look at the sun's face!"

The Reluctant Eagle opened his eyes. But this time he did not look down. He looked into the sun.

It was so near.

He spread his wings.

He flew.

"Three cheers for the Reluctant Eagle!" called Mr Crow and the four-legs and the wings called and whistled and screamed.

"Look at me!" the Reluctant Eagle shouted. "Look at me! I'm flying!"

At the eyrie Mrs Eagle turned to thank Mr Fox, but he was gone. So she poked her husband with her beak.

"Come on."

Together they dropped from the nest, letting the wind lift them up and up until they flew on either side of their son in the bright morning light.

EDOARDO ALBERT

Edoardo Albert was born in London and now lives in North London, where he repairs televisions. His hobby is climbing mountains. The Reluctant Eagle *is his first published story, and he was inspired to write it after a visit to the Scottish Island, Raasay, which is off the Isle of Skye. When he ran out of news in a letter to his friends, Jo and Duncan, who were travelling abroad, he started to write them the story of the Reluctant Eagle. In the original, longer story, the young eagle got his name due to a reluctance to hatch from his egg! It was Jo and Duncan who, on their return to Britain, encouraged Edoardo to enter a shortened version of* The Reluctant Eagle *in the Story of the Year competition.*

Cinderella Knickers

June Burrows

Illustrated by
Julie Anderson

To Amy and Sally.

"Today's Tuesday! Today's Tuesday!" sang Emine's mum from her bedroom.

"Tuesday's recorder! Tuesday's recorder!" Emine sang back.

She rolled out of bed, and across the floor and through the door into her mum's room.

Emine lived with her mum in an old London flat. There wasn't much room, but as there were just the two of them it didn't really matter. They did a lot of things together like roller-skating in the park, visiting people and reading mystery stories. And every weekday morning, they helped each other to remember the things they needed for the day.

Emine went to the local junior school. Like all the other children she had to remember what to put in her school bag each day. She needed her reading book every day, recorder on Tuesdays, swimming stuff on Fridays and shorts and a T-shirt for P.E. on Mondays and Thursdays. There was a time when Emine needed help every day with packing her school bag. Now she only needed an occasional reminder, just as her mum did with her work bag.

On this Tuesday morning the two of them got up and began to get ready for the day ahead. Emine washed and then started the daily routine of finding what her mum called 'suitable' clothes for school. She rummaged around in her drawer, found a vest and then began looking for her knickers. Plain white knickers were what she was looking for but she couldn't find any.

"Mum," she called, "where are all my white knickers?"

"We're a bit behind with the washing," shouted her mum. "I expect they're all in the washing basket. Can't you find another pair somewhere?"

Emine was about to have a temper tantrum, but then she thought better of it.

"There's no P.E. today because it's Tuesday," she said to herself, "so it won't matter which ones I wear."

She pulled a pair of pink knickers out of the drawer and began to put them on. They had a picture of Cinderella on the front. Cinders was wearing two shiny glass slippers, covered in silver glitter. Emine had to admit that the knickers were very pretty, and a couple of years ago she would have longed to wear them. Now, she felt too grown up for Cinderella knickers. Her gran had given them to her for her birthday. Gran still thought of her as a little girl and loved to give her frilly, glittery bits and bobs. Because Emine adored her gran, she would never hurt her feelings by telling her that the knickers were not what she really wanted to wear.

The thing that she really wanted to avoid was the rest of her class seeing the Cinderella knickers, especially Tony Bradshaw. Tony was in Emine's class. Emine liked Tony, but they had been rivals since Infant School. He was always trying to make fun of Emine, tease her and catch her out. This made Emine furious, and sometimes she felt like bursting with anger at the things he said and did. If Tony Bradshaw saw the Cinderella knickers Emine's life would not be worth living!

"Nothing to worry about today though," she muttered. "No P.E. today."

Dressed and ready to face a new day, Emine bounced into the kitchen and began helping her mum with breakfast. She looked at the cereal packets and began to dream about what she would choose if her gran was looking after her. Gran let her eat any cereal she liked, even the sugar-coated ones!

"Now, Emine, I want you to take some of the sensible, wholewheat cereal," said her mum, "not just the sugary ones." The rule was sensible cereal first and then a bit of sugary cereal on top.

"Of course," replied Emine as she sprinkled an extra topping of sugary cereal into her bowl when her mum wasn't looking.

She read the backs of the cereal packets while she crunched her way through her breakfast. There were all sorts of useful things you could send away for if you collected enough tokens, but between them Emine and her mum never quite managed to eat the mountain of cereal needed before the offer ended. Despite this, Emine liked to read about what she might have sent for.

Every morning, as the hands of the clock approached nine o'clock, a panic seemed to grow in the flat. Emine's mum's voice got louder and louder as Emine appeared to take longer and longer to get ready. On the other hand, Emine got more and more bad tempered as her mum seemed to take ages to put on her make-up.

"Come on Mum, you look fine. No one is really bothered about what you look like," grumbled Emine.

"Thanks a bunch!" snapped her mum. "One more word and I'll exterminate you!"

Eventually, teeth cleaned, faces shining and bags packed, they set off together to school. At the school gate, they kissed each other goodbye and Emine's mum walked on to catch a bus to her work.

As Emine walked into the busy playground, she spied Rosie, her best friend. They ran to each other and began to talk. Emine and Rosie were known as the greatest talkers in the school. Heads together, they discussed everything from the latest pop music to parents. Just as they had agreed that school dinners cost too much, Tony Bradshaw arrived on the scene.

"Hey, Emine!" he called. "You've got tomato ketchup on your T-shirt."

He put his finger on Emine's T-shirt. Just as Emine lowered her head to look at the stain, Tony quickly raised his finger and flicked Emine on the nose.

"Made you look, made you stare, made you lose your underwear!" he sang teasingly.

Emine held her smarting nose, too cross to say anything. Anger bubbled inside her as she tried to think of a way to get back at Tony. She stroked her nose and returned to Rosie.

"He's a pain," said Rosie, feeling her friend's hurt pride.

Emine forced a smile.

"I nearly lost my nose, not my underwear!" she giggled.

Later on that day, Emine and her friends tumbled back into the classroom from lunch-time play. Their teacher, Miss Fender, asked the children to sit quietly while she called the register. After the last name was marked in she began to make an announcement.

"Mr Finch won't be using his P.E. lesson this afternoon because he has taken his class on a trip. I said we would swap with him and have P.E. today. He can have our lesson on Thursday instead."

Emine froze. This was her worst fear. Her mind worked quickly.

"But Miss Fender," she said, "we haven't got our P.E. stuff."

"Never mind, Emine," answered Miss Fender gently. "We'll be indoors so we can do it in our underwear."

"I've got my shorts," said Tony Bradshaw smugly.

"That's because you never take them home," snarled Emine.

"Yeah," whispered Rosie. "They're so disgusting, they'll walk home before you take them."

Emine was going hot and cold at the idea of the rest of the class seeing the Cinderella knickers. She closed her eyes and prayed no one was looking as she took off her trousers. Luck was not on her side. Suddenly she heard the enemy.

"Cor, strike a light, look at Emine's knickers!" exclaimed Tony.

The whole class went quiet and turned to look at Emine's knickers. Forty-eight eyes were on her. She tried to fight back the tears of anger which pricked her eyes. Her blood began to boil. Just as she was about to lose her temper and shout something back at Tony, she heard a voice behind her.

"Well, Tony Bradshaw, perhaps you'd like to show us what knickers *you're* wearing today." It was Miss Fender.

"Boys don't wear knickers," sniggered Tony, trying to be clever.

"Surely you're wearing something under your P.E. shorts, Tony," said Miss Fender. "And today we're all going to be doing P.E. in our underclothes."

Tony knew that Miss Fender was being deadly

serious. He also knew that it was only fair for them all to wear their underclothes, even though he'd got his P.E. stuff. Slowly he dropped his shorts. Rosie began to giggle and then the rest of the class spluttered and coughed. Emine raised her head and then she too began to smile through her tears. Tony Bradshaw was wearing a pair of baby's pants with a picture of Thomas the Tank Engine on them!

"I-I-I- couldn't find any clean pants this morning, Miss Fender," he stuttered. "These belong to my little brother and they were all I could find."

Now it was Tony's turn to cry. Everyone felt sorry for Emine and Tony, including Miss Fender. She bent down, gave them both a cuddle and whispered something in their ears. Soon smiles appeared on their faces and they began to laugh.

Later on in the P.E. lesson Rosie whispered to Emine, "What did Miss Fender say to you and Tony earlier on?"

Emine giggled and whispered back, "She said she couldn't show us her knickers because they had a hole in them!"

Rosie's mouth fell open in disbelief. At the same time Emine leapt through the air and Cinderella and her glass slippers flew proudly with her.

STORY OF THE YEAR

JUNE BURROWS

June Burrows was born in Berkshire and now lives in North London, where she is a junior school teacher. She has two girls — Sally, who is six and Amy, who is nine. She enjoys reading, aerobics, dance, and music — she plays the piano, guitar and recorder. She has written educational material and stories, but Cinderella Knickers *is her first published work. She says: "My children's interests have become mine and mine theirs. They give me ideas for my teaching and for my writing. I've always enjoyed reading children's books from all over the world and I love reading aloud to children. All those I have taught and read to have helped me choose books very carefully."*

The King and the 'K'

EMILY SMITH

Illustrated by
ANNA KIERNAN

For Harriet.

There was once a small country called Begonia, which was ruled by a young and handsome king. He was a good king and loved by his people. He was also clever, apart from one thing – his spelling. He could spell simple words like 'dog' or 'log', and slightly more difficult ones like 'clog' or 'frog', but that was about his limit.

For a long time this did not matter, because the king had a chancellor called Wilbraham, who was a good speller. Wilbraham did all the king's writing for him, and checked his letters and laws and proclamations to make sure there were no silly mistakes.

There came a time, however, when the king decided it was time he got married.

"Begonia needs a queen," he told Wilbraham.

"And I know just the right person – Princess Irina of Clematis. I hear she is not only very beautiful, but clever too."

"Yes, Sire," agreed Wilbraham gravely. "The Princess Irina is an excellent choice."

So the king set off for Clematis, with an escort of guards, to ask for Irina's hand.

Now the Princess Irina was indeed both clever and beautiful. She was so clever, in fact, that she had decided she could only marry someone as clever as her – or very nearly, anyway. So she welcomed the king graciously, but explained that before she agreed to marry him, she would have to test him.

"Test me?" said the king in surprise. "Test me on what?"

"Oh, just arithmetic, history and spelling," said Irina. "Don't worry," she added kindly, "the questions are quite easy."

"Well, all right then," said the king. "I'm ready."

"Arithmetic first," said Irina briskly. "What is ninety-nine plus ninety-nine?"

"One hundred and ninety-eight," said the king promptly.

"A thousand take away one?"

"Nine hundred and ninety-nine."

"Nine times nine?"

"Eighty-one."

"Correct!" said Irina. "Now for history. When was the battle of Freesia?"

"1172," said the king.

"Who was the first king of Nasturtium?"

"King Iris."

"Who discovered the continent of Chrysanthemum?"

"Sir John Dandelion."

"Excellent," said the princess. "And now for spelling. How do you spell 'throne'?"

Now it so happened that every day the king passed a door in his castle marked THRONE ROOM.

"T−h−r−o−n−e," said the king.

"Good," said Irina. "I told you they were easy questions, didn't I? Now spell 'crown'."

The king had a box in his bedroom marked in big gold letters with the words ROYAL CROWN. So he shut his eyes, thought very hard, and said, "C−r−o−w−n."

"Quite right," said Irina. "Last question now.

Can you spell 'knife'?"

Easy, thought the king. "N—i—f—e," he declared confidently.

There was a short silence, and then Irina said, "Oh, dear. You've forgotten the silent 'K' at the beginning." She spoke rather sadly because she would have liked to marry the king. He had nice twinkly eyes.

The king's eyes were not twinkling now, though. He was angry. "Are you telling me," he said slowly, "that you're not going to marry me because of one piffling letter — one 'K' that you can't even hear?"

"I'm afraid so," said Princess Irina. "Otherwise there would be no point in the tests, would there?"

Without another word, the king stalked out of the palace. And such was his rage and disappointment that he didn't speak once all the way home. Back at the castle he summoned Wilbraham.

"One letter wrong!" he raged. "One letter, and I've lost a wife! I must be the laughing-stock of Clematis."

"It's an unfortunate outcome certainly, Sire,"

Wilbraham began, "though not −" but the king burst out again.

"One letter − and what a letter too! A silent 'K'! Silent! It's too absurd! Letters have no right to be silent!"

The king brooded in silence for a moment, and then exclaimed, "I've got it! I know what I'm going to do! I'm going to ban it from the kingdom!"

"Ban what, Sire?" asked the chancellor.

"The silent 'K', of course!"

"Well, I could put the clerks to work at once on all the books, crossing it out," suggested Wilbraham.

"I don't mean that!" said the king impatiently. "That's not good enough! No, I'm going to get rid of everything with a silent 'K' in it. And that will put paid to that!"

"A bold approach indeed, Sire," said Wilbraham, "but might I suggest −"

"No, Wilbraham!" said the king firmly. "My mind is made up. We'll start with the knives. People will just have to use scissors or choppers or something. They'll find a way. And then . . . what else has a silent 'K' in it?"

Wilbraham considered. "Well, Sire, there's knights, I suppose, and knaves, knobs, knockers, knitting and —" he gave a little cough, "knickers."

"I want the whole lot out of Begonia by the end of the month!" cried the king.

And so a proclamation went up, ordering all the citizens of Begonia to hand in their knives.

All next day people filed up to the castle. They brought carving knives, fish knives, bread knives, butter knives, paring knives and pruning knives. They brought grand silver knives, humble wooden knives, sharp knives, blunt knives, knives made of gold, brass, bone, ivory and horn. Housewives brought their kitchen knives, boys brought their whittling knives, and old men brought the knives they used for scraping out their pipes.

When the very last one had been handed in, the knives were packed into five huge chests and thrown into the castle moat.

"Well, that's done the knives," said the king with satisfaction, as he watched the bubbles. "Now for the knights."

"Well, you can't throw *them* in the moat," said Wilbraham.

"No," said the king. "They'll just have to leave the country."

"But who'll fight dragons and right wrongs and rescue people?"asked Wilbraham.

"Oh, the soldiers can do all that!" said the king.

The knights were ordered to leave Begonia by sunset the following day. A huge crowd gathered to watch — and what a brave sight met their eyes! First to ride off was the Black Knight, the sun shining on his black armour, the plumes nodding on his black helmet. He was followed by the White Knight, the Red Knight, the Brown and the Yellow Knight. (The Yellow Knight was something of a puzzle as he had never been seen in the land before, nor been known to rescue anyone from anything — not even a cat from the top of a tree.) Their armour chinked and jingled as they rode their proud steeds from the kingdom.

"Good!" said the king, as the last plumes disappeared over the horizon. "Now for the knaves."

So another proclamation went up, ordering

all knaves to leave Begonia at once. But the strange thing was that nothing happened at all. No one left. Not even Jim Jakes, who had been in the stocks three times in the last six months.

"The problem is," said Wilbraham, "that no one *admits* to being a knave."

"Well, it can't be helped for now," said the king. "Let's get on with the knobs and the knockers. I've had an idea about those. We'll do them together."

So right across the land people had to get out their tool-boxes. They then took down lion knockers, fish knockers, eagle knockers, pineapple knockers, nice clean shiny knockers, dirty old rusty knockers, knockers that made a good loud bang, and knockers that hardly made any noise at all. As for the knobs . . . they took knobs off walking-sticks, wagons, chairs, tables, fences and fireplaces. They removed useful knobs, useless knobs, pretty knobs, ugly knobs, and knobs that people had always banged their heads on.

To set an example, the king walked round the castle pointing out knobs and knockers for the

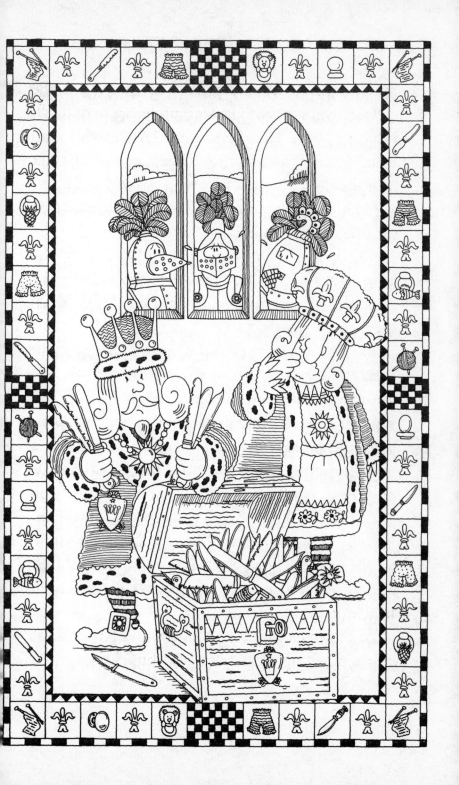

servants to take down. First to go was the huge lion knocker on the castle door. The king himself flung that into the moat.

There was an awkward moment when the king opened his crown box. "Look, Wilbraham," he cried. "Look at those things on my crown! Aren't those knobs?"

"No, Sire," said Wilbraham firmly. "Those are bobbles."

By the end of the day, all the knobs and knockers in the land had been packed into eight cases and dropped into the moat along with the knives.

"The campaign is going well, my good Wilbraham," said the king, pleased. "Tomorrow we shall tackle the knitting."

"Ah," said Wilbraham. "I've been meaning to have a word with you about knitting. The people won't like it. You know how they are about their knitting. They're already grumbling about the knives, the knights and the knobs and knockers. To take away their knitting will make them furious."

Now, in his heart of hearts, the king knew Wilbraham was right. The people of Begonia loved knitting — all of them. Children learnt to knit as soon as they could hold the needles, teenagers knitted, courting couples knitted, mothers and fathers, grandparents and great-grandparents knitted. Lords and labourers knitted, so did merchants and milkmaids, soldiers and sailors, teachers and tinkers. Even Jim Jakes had once knitted a shawl for his mother. They knitted all the things you can think of, and some you can't. They would have knitted chairs and books and bottles if they could.

The king knew this quite well, but he just would not listen to reason.

"I'm sorry, Wilbraham, but it can't be helped. They'll have to weave or sew or crochet instead. And if anyone is caught knitting, I shall fine them ten gold pieces."

The proclamation went out that afternoon, and then indeed there were angry faces across the land. But no one wanted to be fined ten gold pieces, so they all handed over their knitting needles and knitting patterns when the soldiers called.

The next fine day, the king rode round his

kingdom to survey his lands. Usually when he did this, he was greeted in every village by smiling and cheering crowds. But this time there was no such welcome. As he and his guards rode in, backs were turned, shutters were closed and doors were slammed.

Late in the day the royal party crossed a meadow. In the meadow was a flock of geese, and minding the geese was a young goose-girl. The goose-girl was sitting against a tree and – the king couldn't believe his eyes – she was knitting.

He reined in his horse. "Bring that girl over here!" he ordered his men.

When the goose-girl arrived, she dropped a curtsey and said, "Your Majesty?"

"What do you mean by knitting?" the king demanded angrily. "Don't you know there's a proclamation banning all knitting in the kingdom?"

"Yes, I do," said the goose-girl. "But I'm knitting some bedsocks for my grandmother. She needs them, for her feet get very cold at night."

"Do you place your grandmother's feet over

a royal proclamation?" asked the king sternly.

"Well, I do over that one. It's so silly," said the goose-girl, and everyone gasped.

"Shall we tie her up and take her back to the castle, Sire?" asked a guard.

"No," said the king. "Not yet, anyway. Tell me, girl. Why do you think it's silly?"

"Well, Your Majesty, I understand you want to rid the kingdom of everything beginning with a silent 'K'."

"Yes," said the king. "That's right."

"If you do that, you will bring ruin and misery on your land."

"Oh?" said the king. "And why is that?"

"Because then you will rid the country of all knowledge. And where would men and women be without knowledge?"

"Hmmm," said the king. "But is knowledge really so useful? Look at me. I'm king of all this land, but I can't even spell 'knife'."

"Oh, *spelling*," said the goose-girl. "I'm not talking about that sort of knowledge. I'm talking about *real* knowledge — knowing good from evil, truth from lies, knowing who to trust and who to fear, knowing when to speak and when be silent, knowing when to act — and when pass by."

There was silence. And then the king spoke again, in a more kindly voice than before. "But you know, my dear, you disobeyed a royal proclamation. You will have to pay ten gold pieces."

"I haven't got ten gold pieces," said the goose-girl.

"In that case, come to the castle tomorrow, and I will choose one of your geese instead. And be sure to be there," warned the king. "Otherwise you could go to prison."

The next day, the king was woken by a fanfare of trumpets. He quickly got dressed and ran downstairs to find a herald with a message from Princess Irina.

"I come bearing good news from Her Royal Highness, the Princess Irina of Clematis," announced the herald. "The princess, in her great kindness, has reconsidered your proposal of marriage. She has graciously decided to accept your suit — even though you can't spell 'knife'."

"Hmmm," said the king, and the next moment

in walked the goose-girl followed by her flock of geese.

"I've come to give you one of my geese," said the goose-girl.

"Well, I don't want one," said the king.

"Oh!" said the goose-girl, and she began to feel a bit frightened. Would she have to go to prison?

"I don't want you to give me a goose. I want you to give me your hand and be my queen," said the king. He looked into her green eyes. "Will you?" he asked.

"Yes," said the goose-girl. "I will marry you if you stop this silly campaign against the silent 'K'."

"Of course!" said the king. "I was going to do that anyway."

He turned to the herald. "Go back to Clematis," he said, "and tell your princess she's caused a lot of bother in this country and I'm not going to marry her. She may think she's clever, but I think this young lady here is ten times as clever, and I'm going to marry her instead!"

The herald was very surprised, but did as he

was told. When he got home and delivered the king's message, Princess Irina flew into a rage and boxed the poor man's ears. She was last heard of married to a lawyer.

Back in Begonia, everyone was overjoyed that the king had come to his senses at last. The credit for this went to the goose-girl, and they welcomed her straight away as their queen. A good wife, they reckoned, is one who can stop her husband being silly.

Wilbraham was especially pleased to see the end of the silent 'K' campaign. He had been getting very worried about what would happen when the king got round to 'knickers'.

The knives, knobs and knockers were dragged up from the bottom of the moat. They were found to be hardly damaged at all, and returned to their owners. So were the knitting needles and the patterns. The king sent the knights a polite letter (written by Wilbraham), asking them to come back, which they did.

The royal couple had two children, a son and a daughter. Wilbraham made sure they both learnt to spell from an early age. The little prince was never much better than his father, though, and always spelt 'gnome' without the 'G'.

To this day there's no knocker on the castle door (you have to bang with a stick or shout). The door is kept like that to remind everyone of the time the king waged his campaign against the silent 'K'.

EMILY SMITH

Emily Smith was born and lives in London. She has three young children: Kate, Charlotte and Freddie. After completing a law degree she worked first as a legal adviser, then as a reporter on the East Anglian Daily Times *and a reporter and sub-editor on* The Windsor/Slough Express *series. She has also worked casually for a number of magazines, including* Woman's Realm *and* Mother *magazine. She has always been a keen reader and writer, and is a member of Friends of the Earth. The* King and the 'K' *is her first published work. She says: "I tried my hand at a range of writing, but only really got interested in writing for the young when my own children came along. They love books too, and I read to them a lot with one rule — I never read them anything I don't enjoy myself (always excepting my small son's tractor books!)."*